MY BEST AND LAST

JILL RICE

WILDBLUE PRESS
WildBluePress.com

MY BEST AND LAST published by:
WILDBLUE PRESS
P.O. Box 102440
Denver, Colorado 80250

Publisher Disclaimer: Any opinions, statements of fact or fiction, descriptions, dialogue, and citations found in this book were provided by the author and are solely those of the author. The publisher makes no claim as to their veracity or accuracy and assumes no liability for the content.

Copyright 2024 by Jill Rice

All rights reserved. No part of this book may be reproduced in any form or by any means without the prior written consent of the Publisher, excepting brief quotes used in reviews.

WILDBLUE PRESS is registered at the U.S. Patent and Trademark Offices.

ISBN 978-1-942266-55-6 eBook
ISBN 978-1-960332-71-4 Trade Paperback
ISBN 978-1-960332-72-1 Hardback

Cover design © 2024 WildBlue Press. All rights reserved.

Interior Formatting and Cover Design by Elijah Toten, www.totencreative.com

MY BEST AND LAST

This book is dedicated to my Soul Mates,
Pamela Corn Slappey and
Cheri Winham Huff.
Fifty years have gone by in a flash.
I'm looking forward to more great adventures with you.

And to Steven Hodges, my Twin Soul.
I wish I'd known before it was too late.

You Are Worthy of Love.
Open Your Heart to Love Again.
Take A Chance Even Though It May Be Broken.
Because You Also Chance That
Your Soul May Finally Know Its Worth.

CHAPTER 1

The King of Wands represents bold leadership, authority, and calm in the face of adversity.

DANNY

The murder scene stinks. I mean that literally. Something smells so disgusting that I'm gagging into my coffee cup. I've been on the force twenty-eight years and it's rare that I can't handle the smell of a dead body.

"It's too damn early in the morning for this, Biz. I almost puked my Egg McMuffin."

Detective Juanita Bizzell, or "Biz," as she was known around the precinct, gestures to a corner. "Check it out. The rookie CSI tossed his cookies when he saw this." She gestured to the victim.

Biz flips open her notebook. "What we have here is one Paul Michael Davis, age 58, CEO of PMD Brokerage and married to Irina Danova Davis."

"An anonymous tip came in about an hour ago. Someone heard shouting and observed a car racing away from the scene. The tipper said she was a neighbor and identified the victim." Detective Bizzell held up a magazine. "See this?" On the front cover is a photograph of the victim with the caption, "Atlanta's 2022 Broker Of The Year."

I compare the photograph to the victim. "Kind of hard to make a positive ID with that shoe stuck in his eye socket."

"That's not just any old shoe, Danno. That's a Manolo Blahnik."

"So?" I raise my eyebrows and shrug. "What's a Manolo Blah…blah?" I have no interest in women's shoes. Or clothes. Or women period. After my last divorce, I'm done with the "unfairer" sex.

Biz laughs. "Blahnik. A shoe like this runs over a thousand dollars."

"A pair of shoes? On what planet is a pair of shoes worth a thousand dollars?"

"Charlotte asking for more alimony again?" As usual, Biz hits the nail on the head. She is a great detective. Unless she is detecting me, and then she's a pain in my ass.

I picked up a bagged wine bottle from the coffee table. "2009 Chateau Margeaux. That's over a thousand dollars a bottle. Looks like Mr. and Mrs. Davis had very expensive tastes."

Another evidence bag on the coffee table contains a small envelope of white powder. "Coke? Heroin?"

Biz shakes her head. "Could be but I don't think so. The lab boys will have to confirm but I think it's poison." She touches the victim's face with a gloved hand and pulls down his bottom lip. "See that foam around his lips?" She removes a cup from an evidence bag. A small amount of Chateau Margeaux swirls in the bottom of the cup. "Smell that." She puts the cup under my nose.

"Almonds. Cyanide. Where's the wife?"

10 | JILL RICE

Before Biz answers, a loud commotion breaks out in front of the house. Biz nods toward the shouting and banging. "You go. I'll stay here to process the scene."

At the front door, a tall barrel-chested man towers over a much smaller female police officer. The man dwarfs her, but she is solidly standing her ground. Her voice is firm and unyielding, "Sir, step back now or I will detain you."

The man in the standoff with the police officer is Ivan Danovich, the reputed head of the Russian Mafia in Atlanta. A few years ago, I had headed up the team that disrupted a money laundering operation with ties to the Russian mob and several real estate developers. Danovich himself had not been charged thanks to some very expensive defense attorneys. I'm still pissed about it.

"This is my daughter's house!" The man yells, shoving the officer out of the way, "I demand…"

I step up to the door just as the man bursts through, knocking me to the floor. Bowing his chest, the Russian growls, "Izveenee. Sorry, Sorry."

I caught the police officer's eye and shook my head. She nods and holsters her weapon.

"Mr. Danovich," he said, "I'm Detective Daniel Chan." Although Ivan Danovich had at least four inches and seventy-five pounds on me, I forced him back through the door and onto the front porch.

"You say your daughter lives here? What is your daughter's name, Mr. Danovich?"

The angry man squints his eyes, and a slight smirk creases the corners of his mouth as he recognizes me. "Irina Danova," his attitude condescending and defiant.

"Where is she? We need to speak with her. Mrs. Davis's husband has been murdered."

Ivan Danovich is unable to hide the smile that plays across his lips. He mutters, "Durak," and turns to leave.

I grabbed his arm. "Where is she, Ivan? I'm sure you understand our need to speak with her and determine if Mr. Davis had any enemies who might want to harm him."

The mobster breaks my grip and stomps across the porch, kicking over a potted geranium in the process. "My attorney will speak to you."

"Ivan, I don't think you understand the position your daughter is in. I'd really hate to arrest her on suspicion of murder and have her denied bail for being a flight risk. Which I will do if she is not at the precinct by 3:00 this afternoon."

I slam the front door shut, but not before I hear something that sounded like, "Slovich."

I had picked up a little Russian from my informant in Danovich's organization. The Russian had called his son-in-law a fool and me a bastard.

The precinct is on speed dial. "Baker, I need a warrant for the arrest of Irina Danova Davis for the murder of Paul Davis. Stat. Have it on my desk in an hour."

CHAPTER 2

Ten of Wands foretells burdens and the stress of carrying too much.

DANNY

I ease my car into the garage of my Buckhead condo and turn off the ignition. Technically it's my ex-wife's condo. Or rather, my soon to be ex-wife. Charlotte won't sign the divorce papers. We are arguing about everything from alimony to our art collection, to who pays for the cat's psychiatrist. I wish I were kidding. Although the cat does need a psychiatrist. He has a mean streak. The little psychopath pees in my shoes and once scratched me so deeply I needed stitches.

As far as I'm concerned, she can have everything she wants. The condo, the artwork, the furnishings. And, please God, the cat. The only thing not on the table is my cabin. She won't sign the divorce papers until that's hers, too.

Several years ago, I bought a property in a little-known area called Mountain Park. I go there on weekends to fish, lay in the hammock and nap, and chew the fat with the old timers down at the single coffee shop and convenience store. Charlotte had never once been to the cabin. She said it was too "provincial." Yet now that we are getting divorced, it is "adorably quaint and authentically rustic."

I microwave a burrito for dinner but don't have much of an appetite. The image of the leopard print stiletto heel stuck in that guy's eye made me queasy. For all I know the guy deserved it, but still, that's a tough way to go.

When the phone rang early the next morning, I almost didn't answer it. I'm due for a weekend off and I planned to go to Mountain Park.

I roll over and check the caller ID. "What the hell, Biz? I'm on Mountain Park time."

"And a jolly buenos dias to you, too, Danno."

Biz's voice turned serious. "You know I wouldn't bother you without a good reason. Another tip came in. Good thing since Irina Davis has been in Russia for a month visiting her grandmother. You jumped the gun on that arrest warrant, partner."

"Just letting Ivan know who's in charge. If Danovich is involved, a fancy lawyer won't get him off this time. Let's make sure we cross all our Ts and dot the Is. Paul Davis's name came up in the last investigation so I'm digging deeper into his real estate dealings. I'll contact my informant today."

"Then we've got two solid leads. Listen to this—there is some real bad blood between Davis and one of his ex-wives. A "Caroline Cassidy." She is a professor at Peachtree College. La-ti-dah."

With one eye closed I squint at the clock. 6:05 a.m. It was still dark outside. I sighed loud enough to make certain Biz heard it.

"I'm pre-coffee. Just give me the details."

"This Cassidy and Davis owned some property together. Davis bought her out for pennies and then sold it for 16 million. The second tipster says he overheard Cassidy say two days ago that she wanted to murder Paul Davis. Sounds like she's got 16 million reasons to want him dead."

"Who heard the threat?"

A rustle of paper indicates Biz is paging through her notes. "Rolf Eisenstat. Also a professor at Peachtree College. I'm interviewing him this morning."

"Alright, you check out Eisenstat. I'll check out the ex-wife. We'll both take a deep dive into Davis's real estate business and compare notes later tonight."

"Crap." My peaceful weekend in Mountain Park just circled the drain.

Sleep was no longer an option. I made coffee, thinking about the possibility of a new suspect. This murder was not random; it was very personal. Suspect One is a Russian gangster who is known to eliminate anyone who gets in his way. Ivan Danovich would have had Paul Davis killed if he suspected betrayal of any kind. Maybe the guy swindled *him* in a real estate deal.

Suspect Two is an angry jilted ex-wife. A very small percentage of murders, about 4 percent, are committed by women against their partners. It's rare, but it happens. I would have to get a statement from Professor Cassidy before I could determine if she was capable of this kind of violence.

Biz said Cassidy was lecturing at Peachtree College this morning. As I pull into the parking lot there are arrows pointing to the Auditorium. A signboard outside announces today's lecture, by Caroline Cassidy, MD, PhD., is entitled, "Jung, The Shadow, and Archetypes: Revealing Our Greatest Potential."

I have no idea what that means.

The primary interview of a suspect is my strong suit. I have a strong sense within the first 15 minutes if a suspect is guilty. Biz calls it my "Spidey Sense." The other detectives take bets on my hunches. Ninety-seven percent of the time I'm right.

Dr. Cassidy's books are on display and as I peruse them, I realize I have read one of them. Biz had thrown a copy of *Love Hungry* at me a few months after Charlotte asked for a divorce and said, "Read this or else. I'm tired of your moping around and feeling sorry for yourself."

Just because this doctor had written a book that I found helpful didn't mean she was not capable of murder. If anything, my scrutiny of her would be more intense, not less. I don't get emotional about suspects. This woman might have poisoned her ex-husband and shoved a stiletto heel into his eyeball and brain, but she wouldn't have the juice to fool me.

CHAPTER 3

*What lies in the shadow of The Moon?
Secrets, fears, and confusion.*

CAL

I sigh as I drop my notes onto the lectern. I am exhausted from too little sleep the night before and a lot of ranting and raving about the little shit I was married to six years ago.

Marci King, best friend ever, confidant, and occasional partner in crime, had chastised me. "Don't go down that rabbit hole again, Cal. Paul wasn't worth it then and he's not worth it now."

"The man cheated me out of my half of sixteen million dollars, Marce. We bought that property for $35,000. He knew exactly what he was doing when he had his attorney call and offer me $200,000 to sell. You know he had that $16,000,000 deal inked when he was acting oh so magnanimous to make such a "generous" offer over what we had paid."

"Once a liar and a cheat, always a liar and a cheat. I told you that when you first met him."

"I should have listened to you. I would have saved myself a lot of heartache."

Marci smiled smugly. "And?"

"You were right."

It took a lot of cajoling and two bottles of wine to calm me down. Even with the excess wine, I slept fitfully and now do not feel prepared for the seminar I am about to deliver in five minutes.

I look out over the full capacity crowd. A great many of my local book fans who always show up are there. Marci calls them my "groupies." A few of my students are in attendance, angling for a good grade this semester. I give a slight nod to my publisher, standing beside boxes of my books.

Seated alone in the back of the auditorium is an extremely good-looking older man in a suit. Very few men attended my seminars. I write about topics mainly of interest to women: healing after broken relationships, finding meaning in the second half of life, and how to live an authentic, awakened, conscious life.

Some of the women who read my books find "meaning in the second half of life" by divorcing their husbands and creating a life centered around their own interests and dreams. I've had more than my share of threats from angry ex-husbands. I decide to keep an eye on this guy.

Today's topic is a discussion of the hidden power of the Shadow, a concept introduced by Carl Jung and the subject of my most recently published book, *The Shadow Knows*. Jung named the self-defeating stories, fears, and impulses that we keep hidden 'The Shadow.' As long as the shadow remains unacknowledged, it remains in control.

I begin by sharing my personal story. "As a trained Jungian psychologist, I help my clients navigate the losses we face in life: betrayal, illness, death, and financial setbacks. Our Shadow side, the subconscious part of our personality we try to keep concealed, is often revealed during a crisis.

"What do you think happened when I faced a crisis of my own?" I smile at my audience.

"If you said, I dug deep into my darkness and used my training and experience to successfully overcome a serious crisis, you'd be wrong.

"No, I fell apart. I had a mental breakdown that caused me to question everything I thought I knew about myself and life. I had the knowledge here," I pointed to my head, "but not here." I touched my heart.

For the next hour I recount the gut-wrenching story of how my second marriage ended in betrayal and I attempted suicide. "I had worn the mask of good girl, good student, good wife, and good therapist for so long that I was detached from the anger and shame underneath it. Those emotions remained in my Shadow."

I saw the man in the back listening with rapt attention. He was scribbling furiously. Was he taking notes?

"When we take off the masks and bring the Shadow into the Light, we bring the hidden parts of ourselves into consciousness. We are then able to live an authentic life. The shadow is powerful medicine and many gifts, including our personal power, are found within it.

"Understanding who we are, is a lifelong journey. It is the end of the illusion and the beginning of freedom.

"The questions I leave with you today are, 'Do you want to evolve in your spiritual path? Do you want to remember who you are? Do you want to realize your full potential?"

I held up a Tarot card, the Four of Pentacles. "If nothing is risked, nothing is gained. You must be willing to take a leap into the unknown. Are you ready to face your shadow?"

For the next half an hour I answer questions from the audience and then sign copies of my books.

As my publisher and I are leaving the auditorium, I notice the good-looking guy slumped over in his chair. He appeared to be asleep. I part ways with the publisher and approach the man. He sees me and yawns.

"Am I really that boring?" I'm more than a little offended. I sit on the chair next to him.

The man stretches to release the crick in his neck. He reaches into his coat pocket. "I'm here on an official basis."

He flashes a gold badge at me.

The police? Oh God, who's hurt? "Is everything OK? What's going on?" I steel myself for bad news.

"My name is Detective Chan, Dr. Cassidy. I'm here because your ex-husband, Paul Davis, was murdered last night."

There are times I regret that I do not have a poker face. This is one of them. Thankfully, I catch myself before I can give voice to my first thought, "Thank God it's not bad news."

CHAPTER 4

*Knight of Swords seeks truth, moving
forward with assertive action.*

CAL

"I haven't seen or talked to Paul for months. We have been divorced for six years and have no reason to communicate with each other."

The detective appraises my face and my posture. I try to look sorry and sad. I'm not sure I succeed. His eyes narrow.

"I'm sorry that Paul was killed. We did not part ways amicably and haven't had much contact since we divorced. He is a very controlling narcissistic person, and I am glad he is out of my life. I mean, I'm not glad he's dead but if I never see him again, which I won't since he's dead...." My voice trails off.

The more I talk the more flustered I am. *Good grief, Paul is DEAD?*

"I'm making a mess of this." I turn and face him. I read the look on his face—he thinks I'm guilty! I have a momentary vision of him snapping handcuffs on my hands and hauling me off to jail.

"Look, he was abusive and unfaithful. I was so addicted to him it almost destroyed my life. When he left me, I attempted suicide. But whatever issues we've had in the past, I certainly didn't wish him dead, Detective." That was a slight lie. Just two days ago I threw a tantrum like a two-year-old toddler in my boss's office and yelled that I wanted to murder the sorry son of a bitch.

The detective's next words shocked me. "Dr. Cassidy, I must warn you that anything you say can and will be used against you in a court of law. If you cannot afford one, an attorney will be appointed to represent you."

The side of me that is inappropriate in serious situations shows up. I let out a gut-busting bellow, laughing so hard that I fell out of my chair. In addition to being inappropriate, I am also a klutz.

I sit on the floor, laughing. This is surreal. I can't wrap my head around what is happening. Paul is dead and I've just been read my rights. Have I entered an alternate universe?

I hear a commotion behind me. "Cal, are you alright? What happened?" Jim Stanton, my department chair, helps me off the floor. He glares at Detective Chan.

"I'm fine, Jim. I'm fine."

Another lie. I'm not fine. I'm confused and disoriented by the news of Paul's death.

"Jim, this is Detective Chan. He has just informed me that Paul was murdered yesterday."

"What? Is this a joke?" He glares even harder at the detective.

"No, sir. I don't joke about murder. And you are?"

"James Stanton, head of the School of Psychology. Paul was murdered. How? Why? Who would want to murder Paul?"

"Apparently the detective thinks I would, Jim. He just informed me I have a right to remain silent."

I watch as Jim takes a step toward the detective and then stops. He unclenches his hands and retreats. Jim has much better self-control in stressful situations than I do.

The detective looks at me and then at Jim. He appears calm and detached but I note the calculating look on his face. Holy crap, he is wondering if Jim and I murdered Paul together!

"Mr. Stanton, I'm afraid I can't give either of you any details. We are still processing the crime scene." He turns to me. "Dr. Cassidy, I have a few more questions for you."

"Good grief," Jim shakes his head and gives me a hug. "I was just coming in to see how the lecture went. I've got an appointment and I'm late already. You gonna be OK? Do you need a lawyer?"

I shake my head and wave him away. "No, go."

As Jim walks away, the detective asks, "Boyfriend?"

"Oh goodness, no. Friend, boss, and married to my roommate from Med School. Listen, Detective, I am absolutely whipped. I didn't sleep well last night." He doesn't need to know it's because I was having a meltdown over my lying, cheating, and now dead ex-husband.

"I've been on my feet since 6 a.m. I need a huge cup of coffee."

I stand up and walk toward the door, motioning for him to follow me. "Let's go to my office and I'll answer your other questions."

As we walked out of the building, I see Jim ahead of us. He hesitates and turns to look at me. He had warned me a few days ago when I stood in the hallway outside his office to keep my voice down. I did not.

"I'm going to kill Paul. He has cheated me for the last time. I WANT HIM TO DIE A SLOW AND PAINFUL DEATH."

Jim ushered me into his office and closed the door.

MY BEST AND LAST | 23

"Aw, Cal, what'd you have to say that for? Rolf overheard everything you said. You know he's out to get you. He took your last outburst to Dean Minton and I had a hell of a time smoothin' that one over. Shhh... Hold your voice down and pull yourself together.

I exploded. "Did you just shush me? TELL ME YOU DID NOT JUST SHUSH ME."

His concern then and now is evident. He has every right to be worried. He was there six years ago when I found out about Paul's affairs and began a rapid descent into depression.

I feel the threads of sanity loosen. Over Paul. Again.

CHAPTER 5

The Five of Cups suggests loss, regret, and despair.

CAL

I led the detective out a side door and across a parking lot, behind the Anthropology Museum, to my little stone cottage.

The detective stops as I walk up the stone steps, "I'm confused. I thought we were going to your office."

"First floor is my office; second floor is my home." I kick off my shoes as soon as I enter the door. My Golden Retriever picks them up in his mouth and takes them to the closet. I had often wished my husbands were as trainable as dogs. "Good boy," I pat his head.

I pointed the detective in the direction of the kitchen. "Would you please make the coffee? I like it strong. Use two scoops per cup."

From upstairs in my bedroom, I hear the detective rattling around in the cupboards, filling the coffee pot, and clinking cups.

The smell of coffee sends a wave of comfort over me as I change into leggings and an oversized tee shirt.

When I switch on my phone it takes a full minute to stop pinging with missed calls and messages. Twenty-two calls from Marci. She must be frantic if the media is reporting the news about Paul.

I listened to the last message from Marci first.

"Honey, I'm so sorry about Paul. I mean, I know he's a shit and everything and I'm surprised YOU didn't kill him before now." Silence. I hear a sharp intake of breath. "You didn't, did you?" Marci is whispering now. "Shhhhhhhhh, never mind. Don't tell me if you did. Call me!!"

I send a quick text to Marci, making no mention of the fact that there is a police detective downstairs about to interrogate me.

I'm tired, feeling off center at the news of Paul's death, and jittery as hell. I don't have the slightest clue how to convince Detective Chan that I had nothing to do with Paul's death. I don't have much experience with being a murder suspect.

I walk into the kitchen and say, a little too animatedly, "That smells heavenly!"

Why did I say that? Why is the detective making me nervous?

Detective Chan ignores me. He is standing in front of the dripping coffee maker examining one of my coffee cups.

"Dr. Cassidy, mind telling me why you have cups that match the ones found at the murder scene? And I reiterate, anything you say may be used in a court of law."

"This is ridiculous. No great mystery there. Paul and I bought these cups together when we were first married. When he left, I gave him eight and I kept eight."

"Eight. I see." He waves a cup at me. "You have seven cups in your cabinet. Is one in the dishwasher? Or did you break one? Where is the missing cup, Dr. Cassidy?"

I am starting to get angry. I forget for a moment that this man standing in my kitchen suspects me of murdering my ex-husband. "Are you freaking kidding me? I don't keep track of my coffee cups."

I pour a half cup of coffee and add a half cup of cream. The detective looks at my cup in amazement. "I know, most people think how I take my coffee is disgusting."

Detective Chan pours himself a cup. "Got any sugar?"

The threads of sanity snap.

The thought that forms in my mind makes my knees buckle and I stumble into a kitchen chair. I place two fingers on my pulse. It is wild and erratic. I feel nauseated.

It takes every ounce of willpower I can muster not to grab Detective Daniel Chan, kiss him on the lips and say, "Here's your sugar, mister."

Dear God, it has finally happened. I have completely lost my mind.

No, calm down, it is just the shock of the news of Paul's death.

Detective Chan stirs his coffee and the spoon clangs impatiently against the cup. "Sugar?"

Sugar? I can't remember where I keep the sugar. I stare blankly into space as the detective rummages in my pantry for sugar. He pulls out a box of coconut sugar and empties a packet into his coffee. "Oh good god no," he sputters after the first sip. He empties more packets into the coffee and stirs.

He sits at the table across from me.

"Dr. Cassidy, let's...."

"Cal." I interrupt him.

"What?"

"My name is Cal."

MY BEST AND LAST | 27

"Yes, I noticed your friend called you Cal. I thought your name was Caroline.

"It is. In high school I decided to call myself Cal. Much cooler than Caroline." I can tell Detective Chan does not think I am cool at all. He just looks annoyed. I tend to have that effect on many men.

He clears his throat and wipes a small bead of sweat from his forehead. "I prefer for this interview to remain on a professional basis, Dr. Cassidy. This is a murder investigation. Can you tell me where you were the evening of Thursday, April 20th from midnight to about 5 a.m. Friday?"

My gut tightens. I'm afraid I'm going to be sick. I am sweating profusely.

"Is that when...?"

Detective Chan's face is an impenetrable mask.

"I had office hours for my students until 5:00 and a client until 6:00. I picked up dinner for me and Carl at Trader Joe's. We ate, went for a walk, and then I worked on today's presentation.

Detective Chang holds up his hand and checks his notes. "So, you were with Carl all night? What time did you two go to bed?"

"Carl doesn't sleep with me. He has his own bed on the porch."

"Excuse me? Your husband sleeps on the porch?"

"Carl's my dog, Detective." I nod to the Golden Retriever on the living room sofa.

"Carl is an unusual name for a dog."

"Jung."

"Young? Oh, Jung. Carl Jung. Clever."

I must be psychic. I can tell Detective Chan does not really think I'm all that clever.

"Dr. Cassidy, please call your attorney and come to the precinct tomorrow at 11:00 to answer a few more questions."

"I don't have an attorney. I mean, I do for issues involving my book contracts, but I don't have an attorney for something like this." I can't bring myself to say, 'criminal matters.'

"Call your attorney and ask for a recommendation. If you can't make it by 11:00 please call and let me know what time you are coming."

"Tomorrow is Sunday, Detective."

"Yes, it is."

"Isn't it unusual to conduct an interview on a Sunday?"

"Yes, it is."

"You can't possibly think I had anything to do with Paul's murder. That's just crazy."

"11:00 tomorrow morning, Dr. Cassidy."

"What happens if I can't get in touch with my attorney for a recommendation? What happens if the attorney she recommends can't come tomorrow? It's Sunday, for goodness' sake. What if…"

Detective Chan holds up his hand. "Stop." He seems exasperated. Men call it nagging; I call it being thorough.

He pulls a business card from his jacket pocket. "Call Laura Fuller. She's the best Criminal Defense Attorney in DeKalb County." Opening the door he turns and says, "Tomorrow, Dr. Cassidy. 11:00 a.m. He shuts the door with a little more force than I think is necessary.

CHAPTER 6

The Two of Swords indicates you are at a stalemate and facing difficult decisions.

DANNY

As much as I wanted to put Ivan Danovich behind bars, I had to admit Caroline Cassidy was just as likely to be the murderer. She was nervous during the interview and exhibited extreme anxiety about the missing cup. She had no alibi for the time of the murder, and she certainly had motive. She admitted to bouts of mental instability and issues with anger during her lecture. The more this woman talked, the more guilty she sounded.

Except, I was not getting the guilty vibe. Odd. Everything about this woman was a contradiction. A very interesting and attractive contradiction.

I turned the air conditioning on full blast in the car and mopped my forehead with a takeout napkin. Just thinking about this woman made me sweat.

Maybe it's something I ate. Food poisoning. Because I sure as hell am not attracted to a suspect.

I checked in with my informant in Danovich's organization. He has heard nothing about any deals gone sideways involving Danovich and Davis. I ask if there was any chatter about Paul Davis cheating on Danovich's daughter, Irina. Again, nada.

Biz and I both came up empty handed with any shady real estate dealings involving Davis and Danovich. She waived an article from the *Atlanta Journal & Constitution* in my face. The headline read: "Local Real Estate Developer Sells East Atlanta Property For $16 million."

"Looks like that Cassidy woman had sixteen million reasons to kill Paul Davis."

"Yes, it does. Let's get this wrapped up."

CHAPTER 7

The Queen of Cups invites you to be vulnerable in your relationships.

CAL

I winced at the sound of the door slamming shut and sank into the cushions of my sofa. Carl sensed my distress and put his head in my lap.

What in the world is happening to me? Paul's second betrayal and now his death have sent me into a tailspin. I can't do this again.

I dial Marci. She answers and I hear the anger in her voice, "Listen, Missy, how dare…"

I cut her off. "May Day, Marce. I need you now."

"I'll be there in five."

The first thing she says when she walks through my front door is, "Everything's gonna be OK." That's Marci's mantra. When she sat by my bedside six years ago after my suicide attempt, holding my hand and rocking back and forth, I heard her repeat it over and over. I think she was trying to convince herself as much as offering me comfort.

As she hugs me, she whispers, "You didn't kill him, right?"

"The police think I did." When I tell Marci about the visit from a detective and the continuation of questioning tomorrow, she says, "You need an attorney."

She scrolls through her phone, taps a few keys, and sends a contact to me. "Call Laura. She's the best."

I look at my phone. 'Laura Fuller. Criminal Defense.' "That's who the detective recommended. Why do you have the number for a Criminal Defense Attorney?"

"You'd be surprised whose numbers I have in my phone. I cater the best parties in Atlanta."

She makes me start at the beginning and tell her every detail of the visit from the detective. When I mention his name, she nods.

"I know Danny and Biz well. They eat at Serendipity at least once a week. Danny comes in alone more often. I like him. He's a good detective. Biz is a little rough around the edges, though." Marci's restaurant, Serendipity, is the most popular restaurant in Decatur.

"Who's Biz?"

"Juanita Bizzell, his partner."

"His police partner or his *partner* partner?"

Why do I care? How can I be attracted to this police officer? I have no time or space for a man in my life. Where is this coming from?

"Police partner. I don't think Biz's wife would like it if she and Danny were handcuffing each other on the side."

When I get to the part in my story about "freaking coffee cups," I am jolted by a memory: I *did* misplace a cup a few days ago. "Marci, I was with a client when I noticed it missing."

"This could be important, Cal. Which client took the cup?"

"You know I can't share any details with you about that."

"So, change the names and details to protect the innocent. Or maybe, the guilty. Do you realize how weird it is that you notice a cup missing after meeting with a client and that same cup shows up at Paul's murder scene?"

"It's not the same cup. I have eight and Paul has...had... eight."

Marci stares at me expectantly.

"OK, so this client, I'll call her 'Mary,' had an appointment on Thursday."

"Three days ago. The same day Paul was killed."

"Right, so I did my usual thing, check in with the client, how did her week go. Mary is a new client, so I explained how my brand of life coaching works. I always explain why I see clients as a Life Coach, not a psychotherapist, because I use non-traditional methods that are not allowed in clinical therapy.

Marci interrupts. "Yeah, yeah. Get to the missing cup."

"Mary talked about her ex-boyfriend who betrayed her, and she is feeling stuck and angry because she can't get over him."

"Sounds familiar."

"Yeah, it did. Sometimes when a client's situation mirrors my own, I must be extra careful to maintain the focus on *their* healing journey.

"I did a Tarot reading, which now that I think about it, was an odd one. It was the Seven of Swords. It warns about deception and lying. Everything not being as it seems. I told her the meaning of this card and her face turned really dark with anger. Her whole countenance changed. It's like she became a different person."

"Demonic spirit?"

"We don't believe in those. But it did occur to me that something like Dissociative Identity Disorder is a possibility.

"Then she switched gears completely and started to cry and acted the complete victim. It was a disconcerting session. She is the first client that I've never connected with on any level. Before she left, she pulled a little plastic bag out of her purse with a rock in it. Nuummite. A very magical stone. I've been looking for one for a while.

"Anyway, when she handed it to me, I noticed she had bandages on three of her fingers and thumb. She said she burned herself on a hot pan. So, I go get some Lavender Oil for her burns. I'm gone about 5 minutes. I gave her the oil and told her to rub it on at night and in the morning."

"Yes, Plant Witch, I know all about the magic in your essential oils. Stay focused on the demon client."

"After Mary leaves, I go into the kitchen to wash up our cups and there is only one cup on the table where I was sitting. There is no cup at Mary's place. While I'm looking for it, another client calls to schedule an appointment. I simply forgot about it until now."

"Tomorrow, you need to tell Danny about 'Mary' and the missing cup."

"I prefer that I never see Detective Chan again. He's the first man I've felt any attraction to since Paul. It felt too vulnerable. He makes me very uncomfortable."

Marci rolls her eyes, "Yes, because God forbid you are attracted to a decent man."

"I don't think my heart can take another betrayal. Besides, I like being single."

Marci gives me the side-eye. "You just like being in charge. Anyway, I don't think you have anything to worry about with Danny. He is a strictly-by-the-book detective. He would not pursue anything romantic with a suspect."

She pats me on the arm and repeats her mantra. "Everything is gonna be OK. What are the life mottos you plaster all over your books? *What should be, will be. There is no good, there is no bad, there are only teachers.* This will all work out, honey. Me 'n the Universe have your back. Call Laura now. I'll rustle us up some dinner."

Marci dials my phone and hands it to me. As soon as Laura answered, I burst into tears. The pent-up fear and frustration over Paul's betrayal and death, and now being a suspect in his murder are more than I can take. The woman on the other end of the phone waits patiently until I can catch my breath and explain my predicament.

"Give me your address. I'll be at your house at 8:00 tomorrow morning."

Marci is right. What should be, will be. There are no obstacles in our path; the obstacles ARE the path. It is time to practice what I teach.

CHAPTER 8

The Star is a good omen for healing; it represents hope and faith in the future.

CAL

I am too wired to sleep after talking to Laura, so Marci makes a large pot of coffee and a pan of cream cheese brownies.

We stay up most of the night reminiscing. One of the great things about having long-term friendships is the trust level that develops when you face difficult times together. We have seen each other through some tough times with compassion and devotion and so I take no offence when Marci sits me down for a serious conversation.

"You know I love you dearly and will do anything for you. I'd give you a kidney, a lung, and half a liver." She takes my hand, "What I'm about to say isn't easy to hear.

"Jim and Gwen called me today. They, we, have some real concerns about your mental health with all the stress you've been under in the last few days. Jim told me about your meltdown in his office."

I started to protest that I was fine. But I'm not. And I know it. So, I shut up and listen.

"Six years ago, we watched you disintegrate mentally, physically, and emotionally over Paul's betrayal. We didn't intervene soon enough, and we almost lost you because we did not realize how sick you were. You had a mental break then and it looks like you might be heading for another one now, sweetie."

She's right. I was out of control in Jim's office. I threw things and broke the glass in one of Jim's diplomas hanging on the wall. Over Paul. Again.

Then the way I felt today, the sudden attraction to the detective that came out of left field. And what's with the missing cup? Why was the detective so interested in coffee cups?

"I feel like my life went from grounded to chaos in a matter of days. *I am a suspect in Paul's murder.* If even a whiff of that gets out to the news media or the college my reputation is destroyed.

"Everything is spinning out of control and I can't stop it. Just like before."

Marci had literally saved my life then. Well, Marci and Jimmy did. Even though Jimmy was already dead at the time.

When I met Paul, I was recovering from a divorce from a well-known minister of a thriving church in metro-Atlanta. John, my first husband, wanted a very submissive "helpmeet." I was anything but that. I was not meek, silent, or a helpmeet. I was outspoken, irreverent, and according to John, an apostate. I earned that worthy moniker when I came home with a deck of Tarot cards. John ripped them up, burned them in the fireplace, and forbade me to bring any more Satanic devices into our home.

I packed a suitcase and moved out. As I walked out the door, I not only left my husband, but I left his God.

Paul was a breath of fresh air. He had a great sense of humor and most importantly, he did not have a spiritual bone in his body. It didn't hurt that he was devastatingly handsome and sexy (although Marci thought otherwise).

"What do you see in that little turd? He's never gonna marry you, you know. He's a player."

Marci was wrong. We did marry.

Marci was right. He was a player.

There were many signs and red flags over the years that I ignored. When I returned from an out-of-town book tour and found a black thong in our bed, I confronted Paul. He said it was mine. I've never worn butt floss and the last time I was a size small was in the fourth grade. I moved out and filed for divorce. I felt like a failure as a woman, a psychologist, and feminist.

For the first time in my life, I could not find the answers in the traditional psychotherapy I had practiced and taught for decades. I took a three-month long sabbatical from teaching. A week into the sabbatical, at my lowest and most desperate point, I wrote letters to the people I hold dearest and swallowed a handful of sleeping pills.

What happened next is nothing short of a miracle. Maybe not the caliber of the Virgin Birth, but a bona fide miracle, nonetheless.

About the time I swallowed the pills, Marci was awakened in her bedroom by a bright light. It was just a momentary flash, but it scared her. But that wasn't the scariest thing. She heard a voice call her name. "Marci." It sounded like Jimmy's voice, but her husband had died the year before in the line of duty as an Atlanta City police officer.

Marci jumped out of bed and turned on all the lights in the house. She checked the doors. All were locked and chained.

She sat on the living room sofa in her robe and slippers, shaking, trying to make sense of what had happened. "Marci, call Cal." It *was* Jimmy's voice.

Still shaking, she dialed my number. Passed out in my bed in a drug-induced coma, I obviously didn't answer. She dialed three times more, grabbed her car keys, and raced to my house. When I didn't answer the door, she broke a window to unlock it.

She found me sprawled on the bed, unconscious. According to Marci, my breathing was shallow, and my pulse was thready. She took note of the pill bottle and a stack of letters on the nightstand. She opened the one on top addressed to her, scanned it, and called 911. Then she called Jim and Gwen.

Tonight, Marci gently takes my face in her hands and says, "Honey, I don't want a repeat of that night when you tried to…you know."

"You don't have to worry."

I don't really know what happened that night. Maybe the veil between the afterlife and this life was pierced in some miraculous way. Or maybe Marci imagined the light and the voice. I just know that since then I have a renewed sense of purpose and have developed a deep and meaningful spiritual practice.

Marci and I finally climb into bed around 5 a.m., hoping to catch a few hours' sleep before my attorney arrives to prep me for the interrogation.

Before she turns out the light she says, "You've got a choice. You can either give up or rise up."

As I listen to Marci's sweet little puffy snoring, I pray for the strength to rise up. Because it feels like I'm sliding headlong into the black hole once more.

CHAPTER 9

The Devil warns of a toxic relationship and possible sabotage.

CAL

I wake up with a headache on the verge of becoming a migraine. Unrealistically, I am hoping and praying that Paul's murder and the interrogation I am facing are a nightmare. Nope, I'm awake and I hear Marci singing in the kitchen and smell coffee brewing.

"Rise and shine!" I am happy to see Marci carrying a tray laden with coffee and pastries.

"Pain du chocolat! And lemon tarts? You baked this morning?"

"The crew starts baking at 5 a.m. I had them bring these over straight out of the oven." She pats me on the head like a beloved pet. "Special delivery for my little jailbird."

"Not funny," I say with my mouth full of chocolate croissant.

I take a sip of my coffee. She made it just the way I like it. "What would I do without you?"

"Without me you'd be late for your meeting with your attorney. Which is in 30 minutes."

A loud knock on the door downstairs startles us.

"Laura must be early. You get dressed and I'll get her some coffee." The knocking gets louder and more insistent. Marci grumbles as she hurries down the stairs, "Geez, Laura, give it a break."

It's not Laura Fuller at the door. Detective Juanita Bizzell shoves a search warrant in Marci's face.

"Stand aside, ma'am. We have an order to search these premises in connection with the murder of Paul Davis."

"Detective Bizzell, what is going on?" Marci stands her ground, blocking the detective's entry. "Cal is getting dressed and plans to be at the precinct at 11:00 with her attorney."

"Change of plans." Detective Bizzell motions for my friend to move out of the way. "Don't make me move you."

Marci turns and runs up the stairs. "Get out of bed now and get dressed. That's the police downstairs. They have a search warrant."

I leap out of bed, upending the bed tray, spilling the coffee on the bed and the floor. Pastry crumbs fly everywhere. "This is ridiculous. I'm going down there...." I stop, put my hand over my mouth and race to the bathroom, retching.

Marci stands outside the bathroom door with her face pressed against it, whispering, "It's gonna be OK, it's gonna be OK, it's gonna be OK."

"Excuse me, ma'am." Detective Bizzell moves Marci out of the way. "We need to search this room."

"My best friend is in the bathroom tossing her guts and you need to search the flippin' room right now?"

"Yes. Move."

I look in the bathroom mirror: sunken eyes, ashen face, slumped shoulders. I calm myself and open the bathroom door. "It's alright." To Detective Bizzell I say, "Sorry for the vomit smell."

Walking away I add, "Beyatch." Marci grabs my arm and ushers me into my closet.

"Shhhhh! I hope she didn't hear that. Biz has a reputation for being mean and tough as nails."

I drop into a chair in my closet to steady myself from the shock of what I consider an invasion of my home and privacy. I designed the space as a huge dressing room with a comfortable chair, side table, and lots of shelves for shoes, books, and crystals. It is not only a closet but my meditation space.

Detective Bizzell follows us into the closet. She looks around and heads straight for the shelves that contain shoe boxes. She opens one box after another, throwing the lids on the floor and dumping the shoes.

"Detective, if you tell me what you are looking for, perhaps I can find it and you won't have to go to all of this trouble." Despite the migraine and nausea, I speak firmly.

Detective Bizzell turns to me. "Do you have a pair of leopard print Manolo Blahniks?"

"Ummm, yes, but I haven't worn those shoes in years." With effort, I rise from my chair and pull out a step stool. On the uppermost shelf, I pull out a box. "Here you go, Detective."

The detective opens the box and shakes it. Gold tissue paper flutters to the floor. "Where are the shoes, Ms. Cassidy?"

"I honestly don't know, Detective. I can't remember the last time I wore them." *A missing cup and now missing shoes? What in the hell is going on?*

Detective Bizzell tosses the box and snaps open her handcuffs. "I can tell you exactly when you last wore them,

Ms. Cassidy. Thursday night. And you left one stuck in Paul Davis' head."

"You have the right to…"

She may have finished her sentence, but I didn't hear it. I hit the floor in a dead faint.

CHAPTER 10

The Knight of Wands swoops in and takes action.

CAL

I regained consciousness on a gurney being attended by an EMS crew. The EMT stops me when I try to sit up. "Whoa," the woman says. "Take it easy." She helps me sit up and takes my pulse. "When is the last time you had something to eat? "

Marci answers for me. "She had coffee at about 7:30 this morning. And a few bites of a chocolate croissant."

"Lay down." The EMT turns to the man beside her. "Bob, get me a butterfly and saline, please." To me she says, "Your pulse is a little weak and I'm going to test your blood sugar. Just a little prick." She gently lifts my hand and I feel a sting on my middle finger. She swipes the blood into a little plastic white box and sets it aside. "I'm going to start an IV to get your blood chemistry stabilized."

I protest. "I'm already feeling better. Really, I'm fine." Detective Bizzell interjects. "Ms. Cassidy, you don't have a choice in the matter. You are now in the custody of the Atlanta Police Department."

A loud voice booms from right outside my bedroom doorway. "Cool your jets, Biz." I turn my head to see who issued this command. I don't recognize the voice.

A tall woman strides forward and sticks out her hand. "Dr. Cassidy, I'm Laura Fuller. Sorry I'm running a little late." She turns to Detective Bizzell. "Looks like I got here just in the nick of time. Biz, there is no need to take my client to the precinct. Let's get her stabilized and let her rest this morning. I'm booked for the afternoon and tomorrow. How about we come down to the precinct on Tuesday morning? That suit everybody?" I notice she doesn't say it like a question, though. She says it like, "and that's the way it's going to be." I've known her for two minutes and I like her already. She's my kind of control freak.

She stands beside the gurney and pats my hand. "How are you feeling?" I nod in the affirmative. I'm still feeling a little weak. I feel a bruise forming on my tailbone from where I hit the floor when I fainted.

Bob brings over a bag of saline and a needle in a plastic package. Laura holds up her hand. "Hold up, please."

Her eyes search my face. "Do you feel like you need an IV or can we go downstairs and get you some food and tea?"

I'm in awe of my new guardian angel dripping in Chanel and David Yurman. "Food. Tea."

I tentatively swing my legs off the stretcher. Laura puts one arm around me and one arm under me and helps me stand. "You good, hon?"

I navigate the stairs with the help of Laura and Marci. I noticed Detective Bizzell hanging back in my bedroom. Good luck with that. There is nothing in my bedroom that would or could incriminate me. Out of the corner of my eye

I see Detective Bizzell pocketing a small white plastic box. I'm too frazzled to care.

Downstairs, Jim and Gwen are sitting at the kitchen table. Marci must have called them. Jim is cracking his knuckles and looking like he wants to strangle someone. I hope at some point it will be Detective Bizzell.

I lower myself gingerly into a chair with Jim's help.

Laura busies herself with filling the kettle with water and rummaging in the cabinet for tea and cups. "Earl Grey!" she exclaims. "And Vanilla Syrup!" She opens the refrigerator. "Cream! Perfect!" I love the way this woman speaks in exclamation points!

Laura turns to us seated around the table, "Have you ever had a London Fog?" I shake my head, not yet being able to formulate a sentence. "I don't know what it is, but it sounds quite lovely," says Marci.

A few minutes later we are sipping the fragrant tea laced with cream and vanilla. Someone places a croissant in front of me and I take a small bite. After a few sips of tea, I find my voice. "Ms. Fuller, this tea is amazing!" The cup warms my hands and my soul.

"Laura. Just Laura. Feeling better?"

"Much, much better." I look from Jim to Gwen to Marci to Laura. "I feel like I've been on a different planet the last 24 hours. This is surreal. Laura, why do the police think I had anything to do with Paul's death?"

Laura stands up, washes her cup, and sets it on a paper towel to dry. "That's what I intend to find out today." She nods to my friends. "Can you three stay and take care of the good doctor for the rest of the day while I go get some answers?" She walks out of the room before anyone can answer. It wasn't really a question.

The four of us decided to go to Marci's restaurant for brunch. "Let me run upstairs and change. I'll just be a minute." Marci surveys my tee shirt and leggings. "Nah. You're fine. I'm starving. Let's go."

No one speaks on the short walk to the restaurant. I think we are all in shock at the events that just transpired. We slip in the back door and sit at a table in the rear next to the kitchen.

As I settle into the leather banquette, I look up and see Detective Chan and Detective Bizzell on the other side of the restaurant. Detective Bizzell's back is to me. My mouth drops open in surprise just as Detective Chan looks up and sees me. I may have imagined it, but for a brief moment I think I see a smile cross his face; the kind of smile when you see someone you like across the room. Then his face turns beet red, and he looks down, suddenly interested in his food. Detective Bizzell whirls around to see what caused this reaction. She glares at me for a second and then turns around, leans across the table, and says something to her partner, wildly gesticulating. Detective Chan maintains focus on his food.

I will myself not to look in their direction again throughout the entire meal. Angry, confused, and scared, I'm not in the mood to deal with anything but the omelet with roasted vegetables and goat cheese on my plate.

I excuse myself to go to the ladies' room and as I'm coming out and rounding the corner, I crash into Danny Chan. My mouth flies open, and the breath mint I had just popped in flies out and lands on the front of his shirt. "Sorry about that, sir." I picked the breath mint off his shirt and put it back in my mouth. *Sir? I'm an idiot.*

Chan stands in stunned silence for a moment, looking down at his shirt and back to me crunching on the breath mint. His face flushes again. He gives me a half smile, "No problem, ma'am," and proceeds to the Men's Room.

On my way back to the table I'm stopped by Detective Bizzell. Who, along with the entire restaurant, observed the entire breath mint debacle. She leans so close to me I can feel the heat of her anger. "First you murder your ex-husband and then you try to compromise the investigating detective." She gripped my arm harder. "Let's get one thing straight. You picked the wrong cop to mess with."

"Detective, kindly remove your hand from my arm or I will press charges against you." I'm surprised my voice is steady and unyielding. Upon seeing that I'm not intimidated, Detective Bizzell releases her grip.

I step around her. "And Detective, I WILL have your badge if you ever step out of line with me again."

CHAPTER 11

The Seven of Cups signifies strife, indecision, and wishful thinking.

DANNY

I did not agree with Biz's decision to get a search warrant for Dr. Cassidy's home. I thought it was premature. I was still working on the Russian mob angle. We had not yet received any DNA reports from the lab.

"Cassidy and Laura are coming to the precinct on Tuesday for questioning. What's the hurry?"

"Yesterday you said, 'Wrap it up.'" Biz twirled her finger in the air. "This is me. Wrapping."

We agreed to meet at Serendipity after the search. Biz and I eat there a couple times every week. The owner's husband, Jimmy King, was a fellow detective when he was killed in the line of duty several years ago. Marci was struggling to get their little restaurant in Decatur off the ground when Jimmy died. Our entire precinct supports Marci by eating frequently at Serendipity. I eat there more than most. Marci basically feeds me and a few other single detectives every day.

Biz and I had just been served when I saw Marci walk in with Dr. Cassidy and that guy from the lecture yesterday.

It occurs to me that's why Cassidy seems familiar. She is obviously friends with Marci, and I've probably seen her around the restaurant.

Biz claims that when I saw Cassidy walk in, I smiled and blushed. Aside from the fact that I don't "blush," I told her she's nuts.

I was going into the men's room when Cassidy was coming out of the ladies' room, and she bumped into me. It was actually kind of funny. A breath mint flew out of her mouth and landed on my shirt. She picked it off and apologized. Innocent enough, in my opinion.

Biz went postal on Cassidy. I was in the men's room and heard an argument outside. Biz was yelling at someone and when I exited the men's room, I heard, "Detective, I will have your badge if you ever step out of line with me again" and saw Cassidy stomping off to her table.

I told Biz she was way out of line, and she had the nerve to tell me I was one who had crossed the line.

"Dammit, you know me. I never cross a line with a suspect."

Even if she makes me sweat.

CHAPTER 12

The Five of Pentacles asks that you don't let past relationships deter you from trusting a new partner.

CAL

It might have been the Tic Tac incident, or it might have been the bottomless Bloody Marys and Mimosas we consumed at brunch. Whatever it was, we were staggering with laughter on the walk back to my house. "You picked the damn Tic Tac off his shirt and freaking ate it! And then you set Detective Beyatch straight."

"I sure as hell did!"

Jim puts one arm around me and one arm around Gwen. "I knew I didn't like that guy the minute I saw him yesterday. How stupid can he be? I'm gonna knock some sense into that guy the next time I see him, badge or no badge."

I stopped laughing. I've caused too much upheaval in the lives of my friends and I'm feeling a little bit guilty. "This will all be cleared up on Tuesday. I promise."

"Thank God," says Gwen. "You've been acting really weird the last few days."

Jim and Gwen say their goodbyes at the cottage. As they drive away, Marci says, "I'm staying with you again tonight."

"I am fine. Honestly. Go home."

"Not a snowball's chance in hell of that."

We kick off our shoes and cuddle up on the sofa under a mountain of pillows and chenille throws.

"I'm scaring myself. Something in me snapped on Thursday when I found out Paul had sold the East Atlanta parcel. I don't think I've ever been that angry. You should have seen me in Jim's office. I went berserk. Something came over me and for about 24 hours I was consumed with murderous hatred for Paul."

Marci sucks in her breath. "You didn't...You can tell me if you did, you know. Cross my heart it goes to the grave with me."

"If I tell you something, do you swear on Jimmy that you won't tell anyone?"

"You DID kill him!"

"Stop it. I'm serious. What do you know about Danny Chan?"

"Well until today, I liked him. When Jimmy was killed, the Atlanta PD rallied around me. I always thought Danny was nice. He and Biz eat at Serendipity at least once a week." She snorted, "They are paying full price from now on. No more discounts."

Marci is suddenly suspicious. "Why are you asking me about him?"

"I don't know. It's nothing."

"It's obviously something or you wouldn't be asking me about him." Marci narrows her eyes.

I don't say anything.

"You were serious about being attracted to him? He thinks you killed Paul." Marci takes hold of my shoulders, like she is trying to shake some sense into me.

"I can't explain how I feel. Except that it feels like I'm going crazy. I have an unwanted and unprovoked attraction to him and it's freaking me out."

"Did you feel like this with Paul?"

"No, Paul was all lust and the rebound from my divorce with John."

"Never mind. Forget about it. I've met the man once and I felt a slight attraction to him and that's it." I swipe my hands together like I'm dusting them off. "Boom. Done. He's out of my mind."

"Anyway, you are off men. Right?"

"That's not true. I like lots of men. Some men I even love, like Jim. I just don't need a romantic partner. Since my divorce I've been very content with my life the way it is. I've been in two relationships with men who want to tell me what do, when to do it, how to do it, and if I don't do it their way, they get angry."

I didn't dare tell Marci my other insane thought. When Danny looked at me in the restaurant when I first walked in, I felt an energy between us, even across the room. Then, when I bumped into him outside the ladies' room, there was something in his eyes that flashed momentarily, almost like desire.

"What? What's that moony-eyed look on your face for?" Sometimes I hate that Marci knows me so well. There is no keeping a secret from her.

Marci waits. I sigh. She will get it out of me eventually. "I think…he likes me, too."

"OH HELL NO. You have lost your mind. He is probably going to arrest you tomorrow for murder." She picked up her phone, muttering to herself. "I'm calling Jim. You need some anti-psychotic drugs or something."

I took the phone and ended the call.

"What I need is something to take my mind off all this insanity."

I light the gas logs in the fireplace and tune up one of our favorite movies on Netflix while Marci makes coffee and heats up leftover cream cheese brownies. Marci and I are suckers for romantic comedies. And cream cheese brownies. Probably why neither of us are a size 8 any longer.

I'm into my second brownie before long. "This is divine. If I died right now, I'd be happy."

"Well, you may just get your wish with the death penalty for murder thing you've got going. Do you want 'She Died Happy' on your tombstone?"

I love that nothing is sacred with Marci.

Halfway into the movie, Marci grabs the remote and puts the movie on pause.

"Twin Souls."

"Yes. How astute of you. Harry and Sally are Twin Souls. Now, shut up and turn the movie back on."

"No. It just occurred to me, this instant attraction between the two of you. You're Twin Souls."

"There is no attraction. Now *you've* lost your mind. Turn the damn movie back on."

Marci rifles through my bookshelf until she finds the book she wants. "Just listen."

"Twin Souls will experience an intense reaction or attraction to one another when meeting for the first time. There is a deep emotional and physical connection but there is also a spiritual connection."

"You're crazy."

She continues reading. "Twin Souls often feel a sense of completeness that can feel like 'home.'"

"You are delusional."

"Holy Cow, listen to this," Marci says excitedly. "When you meet your Twin Soul you will be drawn to them physically and will feel an emotional charge between you."

MY BEST AND LAST | 55

"Oh shit."

"Wait, there's more. According to this, you and I are Twin Souls, too! Best Friend Twin Souls Forever! That's a good thing, right?"

I don't answer. I'm still processing the Twin Souls idea.

Marci turns to me, "Do you think we could have been married in a former life?"

I can't think about Twin Souls. *Please don't let her be right.*

Marci ignores my silence. "IF we were married, I was the cute, smart one and you were the controlling, bossy one."

CHAPTER 13

Conflict and power struggles take the forefront with the Five of Swords.

DANNY

On Tuesday morning we closed the investigation into Ivan Danovich as a suspect in the murder of Paul Davis.

"There is no evidence that Danovich killed Davis, Danny. Your informant alibied Danovich for that day and said he has heard no chatter about Ivan being involved." Biz was getting more frustrated with me by the minute.

"Why are you still harping on the mob angle? Despite what you say, I saw how you looked at Cassidy on Sunday."

"Drop it. Caroline Cassidy is a suspect in this murder investigation. Period. End of story."

"You're blushing again."

"Dammit, Biz, I said drop it. Talk about crossing the line. Just stop with the accusations."

Biz looked taken aback. "Whoa. Didn't mean to get you so upset about something you say is non-existent."

Crap. Biz can read me like a book. I retreat into the precinct kitchen.

I can't stop thinking about that damn woman. I even had a dream about her last night. It was *that* kind of dream. I woke up soaked in sweat.

Nothing like this had ever happened to me. I have always maintained strict professionalism with colleagues, court personnel, and of course, with suspects and perps.

Yesterday, I called a friend of mine. Steve is a therapist, and I knew he would keep our conversation confidential even though I'm just a friend and not a patient.

I explained that I had an inappropriate attraction to someone. "Why would I be attracted to someone if it would not be right for us to be in a relationship?"

"Lots of reasons. Why are any of us attracted to one person and not another? In your case, it may be the forbidden aspect of it that is fascinating. Or maybe you've just been single too long and this is the wrong person who came along at the right time."

I didn't think any of these scenarios applied to me.

"Usually, we are attracted to someone who shares the same values and beliefs. You know, someone we have something in common with. You say you just met this person a few days ago and it was an instant attraction?"

"I can't explain it, but yeah."

"Well, my friend, maybe she's The One."

"The One? That's some fairytale fantasy. Doesn't happen in real life."

"Chemistry, magic, soul mates…it does happen, Danny. If you are feeling a strong attraction to someone, you need to ask "why." What missing part of you is she completing?

What need does she fulfill in you? Tell me—what is it about her that you find captivating?"

"She's brilliant—well educated but down to earth. She's funny, intelligently sarcastic. She's attractive in an organic, natural way. And she's got moxie."

"She sounds wonderful. I can see why you are attracted to her."

"You're not really helping much."

"You say you know what you must do, which is not pursue a relationship with her. So, don't worry about your feelings. Feelings originate in our ego mind. Feelings tell us all kinds of lies. You know the right thing to do. And I'm confident that's what you'll do. You are a man of impeccable integrity."

Biz poked her head through the doorway. "Lab guys want to see us in the conference room."

Ramesh was waiting for us. He handed Biz a manilla folder. "You've got yourself a suspect, guys."

Biz scanned the document. "Ha! I knew it. Cassidy is a DNA match to the shoe and the cup. Her fingerprints match the prints on the plastic envelope the poison was in. Boo-yah!"

I had been holding my breath while Biz read the lab results. Dr. Cassidy's fingerprints were in the system because she worked for Peachtree College. How did they make the DNA match?

"Ramesh, did you have a blood or saliva sample to match to the crime scene?"

The lab tech consulted the report.

"Yes, we did. We had a blood sample from the suspect."

I looked at Biz. She would not look at me. She was studying the staple on the lab report.

"Biz?"

"It's a match, Danny. Drop it."

"Congratulations, Biz." I left the room and went to my desk. I opened my department email and typed a letter of resignation to the Commander.

I am seriously screwed. I let my feelings for this woman interfere with my better judgment.

On second thought, I deleted the letter. The DNA and fingerprints are a match. I look at my watch. 11:00. Time to nail a suspect.

CHAPTER 14

The Tower portends sudden change, chaos, and upheaval. This is a necessary step in your journey.

CAL

My hands are clammy as Laura and I climb the steps and enter the double doors of the Virginia Highlands precinct.

Everything will be OK. Everything will be OK. Everything will be OK.

I feel sick to my stomach.

Laura places her hand on my back as we step over the threshold. "Stay calm, Cal. You've got this." *From your lips to God's ears, I prayed.*

Laura greets the police sergeant at the front desk like he was an old friend. "Hiya Eddie, how's it going? Listen, my client, Dr. Cassidy, is here to speak with Detectives Chan and Bizzell. Can you have Sue Ellen get her prints and then escort her into Room C? I'll let Danny and Biz know we're here."

"Sure thing, Ms. Fuller."

Laura instructs me, "Wait here until Sergeant Knight comes to get you. I'll meet you in the interrogation room. I want to have a word with the detectives."

Eddie—Sargeant Eason—picks up the phone and punches a few buttons. "Sue," he said, "got some fingers for ya."

A few minutes later Sgt. Knight ambles down the hallway. "Ms. Cassidy, come with me." She leads me down the hallway and through a dreary squad room. There are several police officers sitting at their desks, doing paperwork, or talking on the phone. Detective Chan is seated at one of the desks, typing on a computer. I know he saw me enter the room, but he completely ignores me as I pass by.

I tell myself this will be over in a few minutes. They'll realize they have made a mistake and I'll be home in time for a late celebratory lunch with Marci."

Sgt. Knight stops at a desk in the back of the squad room and motions for me to sit down. The sergeant opens her laptop and presses a few keys. She slides a tablet over to me.

"Left hand, please." She places my fingertips one at a time on the pad, checking her computer screen after each impression. "Right hand."

When she finishes, she stands up and says, "Follow me." She never meets my eye or cracks a smile.

We go down another hallway. She stops about halfway down, opens a door, and walks away.

To my great relief, Laura was sitting in one of the chairs around the table. She is having an animated conversation with a man in a suit whose back is to me and Detective Bizzell, who is sitting at the end of the table. The light banter and laughter cease when I enter the room. The smile on Detective Juanita Bizzell's face is replaced with thinly disguised hatred.

Laura rises walks over to me. She gently places a hand on my elbow and guides me to the seat beside her. "Would you like some water, Dr. Cassidy?"

"Yes, please, no ice."

Detective Bizzell snorts. She looks up at the two-way mirror and says, "Hey Franco, please bring our guest some water, chilled, no ice, in a frosted goblet." She turns to me, "Anything else? Caviar and toast points?"

"Biz," chastises Laura, shaking her head.

The two women are obviously well acquainted. *Maybe that will work to my advantage.*

A moment later the door opens, and a uniformed officer hands me a paper cup. I take a sip; it is tepid tap water. I smile at Detective Bizzell, "Thank you, Detective."

No one speaks for the next few minutes. Detective Bizzell is busy making notes on the inside cover of a manilla folder full of papers. Laura checks her mobile phone for messages and then discreetly places her hand on my knee to stop the nervous tapping of my foot that is shaking the table.

I sit up straight in my chair. I cross one leg over the other and fling my arm over the back of Laura's chair, telegraphing to Detective Juanita Bizzell that I am relaxed and comfortable because I am, after all, innocent. I contemplate suing the police department for false arrest. Specifically Detective Bizzell. And maybe I'll throw in Detective Twin Soul for good measure.

He enters the room carrying a box, putting it on the floor between his and Biz's chairs. I can't help it; I inhale slightly when I see him. I don't think of him as "Danny" any longer. He is Detective Chan and like Detective Bizzell he is my adversary.

"Sorry to keep you waiting," Detective Chan says. He avoids my gaze. "Just conferring with CIS and confirming a few things."

MY BEST AND LAST | 63

He turns to Biz. "You've apprised Dr. Cassidy of her rights?"

Biz nods, "Ready to rock and roll."

Chan turns on the recording device. "This is April 25, 2023. Detectives Daniel Chan and Juanita Bizzell interviewing Susannah Caroline Cassidy. Also present is Laura Fuller, Dr. Cassidy's attorney, and Aaron Carter, Fulton County DA."

He finally looks at me. His face is unreadable with no hint of emotion or kindness.

"Dr. Cassidy, we appreciate you coming in to clear up a few inconsistencies regarding the murder of your former husband, Paul Davis. Would you mind telling us how you learned about Mr. Davis's death?"

I take a sip of water and clear my throat. "I learned about Paul's death from you, Detective. You came to a seminar I held at the college on Saturday, April 22."

"That would be Peachtree College?"

"Yes, that's right. I am employed by Peachtree College."

Chan continues. "You didn't hear about it on the news, or a friend didn't call to tell you what happened?"

"No." I am thankful my voice is strong and clear. "I don't watch the news."

Bizzell interjects. "What about phone calls from family or friends who might have seen it on the news? Surely someone saw it and contacted you."

"No, when I'm preparing for a lecture, I turn off my phone. I had a drink with a friend at my house around 5 and she left around 6:30. I turned off my phone and prepared for the seminar. On Saturday, after the seminar when I turned on my phone again, I had a million frantic messages from friends and colleagues. But by then Detective Chan had already informed me about Paul's death."

Detective Chan resumes the questioning. "When was the last time you spoke to your late husband?"

"Ex-husband," I correct him. "It would have been in October of last year when he called to ask if he could buy my share of the property we owned together in East Atlanta. I said I would have my attorney contact him to arrange the sale. My attorney handled the transaction from that point with power of attorney and Paul and I didn't have any reason to speak after that."

Detective Bizzell opens the manilla folder and takes out several sheets of paper. "So, you are saying you have not had any telephone conversations with your ex-husband for six months. None?"

"Yes, Detective Bizzell, that is exactly what I am telling you. Paul and I have not spoken since October."

Detective Bizzell slides the papers across the table. "Perhaps you can tell us why Mr. Davis's phone records indicate that you and he talked several times a week, with the last phone call being two hours before his death."

"That's impossible. You and your phone records are mistaken. I will repeat, I have not spoken on the telephone, in person, by email, or any other method, to Paul since October."

"These are not 'our' records, Ms. Cassidy. They are AT&T's records."

Laura reaches for the papers. She shows the top sheet to me. There are many highlighted lines, all calls to the same number. "Is this your phone number?"

Without looking at the paper I say, "No, it's not," but when I look at the paper, I see my office telephone number. The calls were incoming and outgoing. I recognize Paul's home telephone number. "This is literally impossible. I have not called Paul and he hasn't called me. This is a huge error."

"Oh, I think not, Ms. Cassidy." Bizzell picks up the paper and waves it. "According to these records, you and Mr. Davis spoke three or four times a week. What did you two talk about? Did his wife know you were in contact?"

A tiny trickle of sweat forms at my temples and the base of my throat. My armpits are sweating profusely. I feel flushed. I locked eyes with Laura. I need her to believe me.

"I swear I have not spoken to Paul since last October. These records are wrong. They're fake." Detective Bizzell snorts and slams her hands on the papers in disgust.

"Dr. Cassidy, where were you on the night of Thursday, April 20, from midnight to 5:00 Friday morning?" It was Detective Chan who asked the question. I ignore him. I point to the piece of paper on the table. I can't let this go. "This is a mistake. These are wrong. Paul and I haven't spoken since October."

Detective Bizzell raises her voice. "Detective Chan asked you a question, Ms. Cassidy. Where were you on the evening of April 20th?"

"I was home, preparing for Saturday's seminar." Sweat is pouring down my back now. "I've already told you this."

"Was anyone with you?" Detective Bizzell glances at her partner and says sarcastically, "Other than your dog?"

That's it. I've had enough. I am hot and sweaty, thirsty, and a little bit dizzy. And frustrated as hell. I raise my voice to match the decibel and timbre of Detective Bizzell's. "I have already explained to you that I do not like distractions when I am preparing for a lecture. I was home alone." I slam my fist on the table. "My television was off; my fucking phone was off. I worked on the presentation until midnight and then went to bed."

"So, you have no alibi for the evening?" I want to kill that bitch.

Finally, Laura speaks up. Apparently, she either thinks I'm doing fine by myself, or I am a lost cause. "Asked and answered, Biz."

Bizzell continues. "When was the last time you were in Paul's home?"

Laura notices the sweat running down my cheek and says to Detective Chan, "Danny, can we get Dr. Cassidy another cup of water?"

Detective Chan nods at the two-way mirror.

Taking a deep breath I say, forcefully, "I've never been in the home that Paul lived in. When we divorced six years ago, he moved out of the home we shared and bought the house in Virginia Highlands. I've never had occasion to visit Paul there."

Detective Bizzell feigns a surprised look. "Really? You've never been to Paul's home?" She reaches into the box between her and Chan and pulls out a plastic evidence bag. "Dr. Cassidy, do you recognize this cup?"

She takes the cup from the bag and places it in the center of the table.

"Yes, I have a set of cups just like this at my office. They are from a gift shop in Decatur." I look pointedly at Detective Chan. "We've discussed this before."

"Are you missing any?"

"As a matter of fact, yes, I am missing one cup."

Chan held up his hand. "Hold on, Dr. Cassidy. I questioned you about a missing cup and you said, verbatim, 'I don't keep track of my coffee cups.'"

"You are correct, Detective Chan. I said that at the time you questioned me. Since then, I have counted my cups, searched my home and office, and determined that one is, indeed, missing. I think a patient stole it." I try not to sound snarky but fail. "I officially amend my previous statement."

"Dr. Cassidy, we found this cup in Paul's house."

"Well, that makes sense. As I have said before, he has eight of them."

Detective Bizzell plays her trump cards. "Does it make sense, Ms. Cassidy, that your fingerprints and DNA were found on the cup in Paul's house? The house you say you've never visited. Your fingerprints were on the plastic bag that the poison was in. The poison that killed Mr. Davis. Your fingerprints were also found on the bottle of wine that you two shared that night."

The detective smiles triumphantly as she pulls a plastic bag with a shoe in it out of the box and slams it on the table. "And it was your Manolo Blahnik that was shoved through Paul's eye socket." Bizzell tosses a color photograph on the table. Paul is lying on the floor with a high-heeled shoe sticking in his head.

Detective Chan snatches the photograph from the table, and I hear Laura shout, "What the hell, Biz? That was uncalled for."

The interrogation ends at that moment when I throw up all over the table, the cup, the shoe, the phone records, and Detective Bizzell's polo shirt.

CHAPTER 15

THE HANGED MAN

The Hanged Man asks that we let go of old misconceptions, take time for reflections, and see things from a new perspective.

DANNY

What a cluster. Biz has vomit all over her and is headed to the showers. I caught up with her.

"Fucking bitch threw up all over me."

"I don't think she did it."

"Of course you don't, Romeo. But I've got news for you, she did."

"She did not act guilty in there. Did you see how she reacted when you threw that photograph on the table? She was completely shocked. She had never seen that before."

Biz turns around. I've never seen her so angry with me. We're like that perfect married couple that never fights.

Until now. "Get your head out of your ass, Danno. It'll get you in trouble if you don't."

My mind is working overtime. If Danovich didn't kill Paul, and Dr. Cassidy is innocent, who killed him? Who framed Dr. Cassidy for the murder and why?

CHAPTER 16

The message of the Seven of Wands is clear: it is time to stand up for yourself. You can handle any challenges that come your way.

CAL

"You seem to throw up and faint a lot." Laura hands me a Diet Coke.

"Always have. I have a weak stomach and chronic hypoglycemia. You should have seen me in med school. The attending made me carry a barf bag every time I rounded with her. My stint in the ER was a nightmare—for me and the patients I threw up on. It's one of the reasons I decided to go into Psychiatry. No bloody gaping wounds, no bones protruding through skin, no dragging a needle through lacerated flesh." I shudder just thinking about those med school memories.

We are now seated in Room B, since Room C was being thoroughly cleaned by a HazMat team. Detective Bizzell is in the locker room showering.

"Laura, that photograph…oh my god, that was horrible. I've avoided listening to or reading reports about Paul's death because Marci said it was gruesome. Was it really *my* shoe that…"

Laura speaks softly. "DNA tests confirm it is your shoe. It is your fingerprints on the cup and wine bottle on Paul's coffee table. Your prints on the bag of cyanide that was found at the scene."

"That's impossible. I have never been to Paul's house. Never."

"It gets worse. One of your colleagues from the college claims he heard you threatening to kill Paul the morning of the murder."

Shit. Rolf. "That part is true. I was angry."

Laura raised her eyebrows. "The police received an anonymous tip Friday morning that a person of your description was seen leaving Paul's house at 4:00 a.m. that morning. A car with your license plate number was parked in his driveway from midnight to 4:00 a.m. They are trying to locate the witness now.

"That is definitely not true. I was not at Paul's house Friday night."

"Then think—who would want to plant evidence and frame you?"

"Frame me? Nobody! That's ridiculous."

"Cal, either you killed Paul, or someone is framing you. Those are the only two explanations for the presence of your DNA at the crime scene. Tell me about your divorce. Was it amicable?"

"Absolutely not. Same old story: boy and girl fall in love. Boy cheats, girl finds out, girl lays down an ultimatum, boy leaves and sets up house with his lover.

"I was devastated." I sigh and look down. "I sort of got a little off center and threatened Paul. I stalked him and the girlfriend."

I continue in a low voice. "Tossed a few rocks through his window. Egged his Jag."

Laura looks surprised.

"I created a scene at the girlfriend's workplace, and she filed a restraining order. That's when I tried to kill myself.

"Look, I am not proud of how I handled myself six years ago. I acted impulsively and immaturely. I am horrified by my past actions. Ironically, that experience is what put me on the spiritual path that I follow today. I faced my inner demons, and let me tell you, they were nasty. In the end, it was the catalyst that changed my life.

"I realized I have the power to create my own destiny and everything that happens to me actually happens for me—to further me on the path to enlightenment. I wrote a few books that turned out to be very popular and I have created my dream life."

"What about this real estate deal gone bad between you and Paul?"

"I found a piece of land in East Atlanta off Moreland Avenue 10 years ago. I convinced Paul it would be valuable one day, so we bought it together. When we divorced, it was an asset we forgot to divvy up. When Paul wanted to buy out my share, I just signed the papers my attorney sent to me.

"I never dreamed Paul would deceive me. I know, stupid of me since that wasn't the first time he'd been dishonest. He cheated on me once, why did I think he wouldn't do it again?"

Laura closes her notebook, snaps the cap onto her Mont Blanc, and stores both in her briefcase. "The police have all the evidence they need to indict you for Paul's murder. How fast can you get your hands on $100,000 for a cash bond?"

"A hundred thousand dollars? Do you think they are going to arrest me?"

"They are preparing the indictment now. Detectives Chan and Bizzell cross their Ts and dot their Is. They don't bring a suspect in for questioning until they have enough to get an indictment. We'll be going to the arraignment shortly and I know the judge won't approve anything under a million dollars for capital murder. You must put up 10% of that in cash as bonds and surrender your passport. I'm confident I can get you released until trial."

Indictment? TRIAL?

"How liquid are your assets?"

What the f....

Detective Bizzell opens the door, dressed in a clean shirt and khakis. "Ladies, it's show time. Vamanos."

She is grinning like a Cheshire cat.

CHAPTER 17

*The Justice card stands for truth. Stay true
to yourself and act with integrity.*

CAL

To date, the greatest horror and humiliation of my life is being transported to the courthouse in the back of a police cruiser. Laura directs Detective Bizzell to take me around to the back entrance because "the AJC, CNN, and FOX are out in full force at the front of the courthouse." Once more I wonder about this woman's mojo. Her "requests" sound more like edicts.

I'm certain Detective Bizzell could have been a tad gentler with the cuffs, but I let it slide. I did throw up on her. Not on purpose, though she might not realize that.

At the courthouse, she takes me by the elbow and steers me through the courthouse door. A court officer meets us, and I am released into his custody.

I sit at the defense table with Laura. The DA who had been present at the interrogation, Aaron Carter, is seated at the other table. Detectives Chan and Bizzell are seated directly behind him.

The judge enters the room. "Crap," Laura swears under her breath. I think I heard Detective Bizzell chuckle.

"All rise. The Honorable Gretchen Jackson presiding."

Judge Jackson is one of the tallest and most regal women I've ever seen. She looks fairly familiar; maybe I'd seen her at some of the college's fund-raising events.

Judge Jackson nods to the ADA. "Mr. Carter, are the people ready?"

"Yes, your Honor, we are."

The Judge turns to Laura. "Ms. Parker?"

"Still go by Fuller, Judge."

Recognition floods my mind. Laura Fuller is married to Elizabeth Parker, current Governor of Georgia. It was a big deal when Governor Parker was elected as the first female and first gay Governor of a Bible Belt state. It was a bigger deal when she married her longtime partner a few weeks ago.

Now it made sense why Laura wields so much power around the precinct and courthouse. No one is going to intentionally step on the toes of the wife of the Governor. As for the Judge, I realize why Detective Bizzell chuckled when the Judge approached the bench. Judge Jackson is known as the toughest judge in the city on crime. "Maximum Jackson" is her nickname.

"We are asking that Dr. Cassidy, a professor at Peachtree College and a long-standing member of the community, be released on her own recognizance."

"The people object, Your Honor." Aaron Carter pounds the table for effect. "This crime was unusually violent and there is a history of violence perpetrated by the suspect on the victim."

Well, it was just a few eggs and rocks. Nothing serious. But there was stalking and that pesky restraining order.

"In addition, Your Honor, we have a credible witness, in fact, a colleague of Dr. Cassidy's, who will testify that he heard Dr. Cassidy threaten to kill Mr. Davis the very day he was viciously murdered. We are locating an additional witness who can place Dr. Cassidy at Mr. Davis's home at the time of death."

Judge Jackson peered over her bifocals. "Ms. Fuller?"

"Judge, you will note in the folder on your desk several depositions by colleagues and supervisors of Dr. Cassidy and a statement of support from Peachtree College. We will prove these accusations to be untrue and Dr. Cassidy will be exonerated of all charges in short order. That folder also contains Dr. Cassidy's passport, Your Honor. We will fully cooperate with the court to have this matter brought to trial and dismissed as soon as possible."

Judge Jackson reviews the pages before her for several minutes. It seems like an eternity to me.

"Five million dollars bail and released ROR." She looks pointedly at Laura Fuller. "Counselor, don't make me regret this."

"Your honor, if it please the court...."

Judge Jackson cut off Aaron Carter's plea. "It does not please the court, Mr. Carter." She bangs her gavel. "Next case, bailiff."

I confer with Laura in a small anteroom just outside the courtroom. A tough-looking biker is also present in the room.

"Cal Cassidy, this is Eagle Finnegan. She is the best PI in Atlanta. She is going to be your angel, your best friend, your miracle worker, and your savior." Eagle shakes my hand.

"Dr. C, I'm going to crawl so far up your life that you won't need a colonoscopy for the next 10 years."

Wow. Subtle.

Laura gets right down to business. "How long will it take for you to get a check to me for $500,000?"

"Half a million? I thought you said it would be $100,000."

"Don't look a gift horse in the mouth. You are not in jail. You are spending every night before the trial in your own comfy bed. Gretchen did me a favor. I now owe her a big one. If you need time to pull together the funds, you'll have until end of the day." She pulls a card from her pocket. "This is the bondsman's information."

I take my checkbook from my bag. "I'll just give you the check now."

"Academia pays a lot better than I imagined." Laura looks impressed. She doesn't need to know that I have just emptied my 401K and entire savings to post bail.

"Well, I've written a few books that are popular."

"You're being modest. Your books are bestsellers."

"You've done your homework, Counselor."

"I always do." She smiles and I can't tell if it is intended to be comforting or calculating. The answer becomes crystal clear with her next question. "Did you kill Paul?"

"Are you kidding?"

"No, I am not. I'm serious. Did you kill him? I need to know how to prepare your defense."

"If you think I killed him I will find another attorney."

"You haven't answered my question."

"NO!"

"But you thought about it after you found out he cheated you out of your share of 16 million dollars."

"Damn right I did. I thought about it after I caught him cheating, too."

Laura claps me on the back. "Alrighty then. If you were guilty, you would have denied thinking about killing him." She turns to Eagle. "Do your thing. We don't have a lot of time to waste."

"On it, boss."

"Before you leave, I need another check for $50,000. Eagle is very good at what she does, and she spreads a lot of money around town to get the information she needs."

"No problem." I write another check. I'll have to move some funds around to cover it. I make a lot of money from book sales but most of it goes to a charitable foundation I created to fund educational scholarships and housing for victims of domestic violence.

"Thank you. This has been the craziest three days of my life and I appreciate everything you've done for me."

"Cal, I believe you are innocent, but this is for Danny. He's a great guy and my favorite ex-husband."

Ex what? Good freaking grief.

"Be at my office at nine in the morning. We need to go over the evidence and figure out who is setting you up."

Laura walks out of the anteroom before I have a chance to respond.

CHAPTER 18

The Seven of Swords warns of self-deception and lying.

JULIET

Juliet Morrison was enjoying a late afternoon lunch with friends. It was a gorgeous spring day and they had chosen a table on the covered patio.

"I've heard the food at this restaurant is amazing! Why don't we all order something different and share it."

Darryl agreed as long as everything was gluten free.

"I came here just for the truffle pizza and that's what I'm going to have." Marlene took out a cigarette and started to light it.

"You can't smoke here, Marlene! This is a non-smoking restaurant. Where have you been for the last 25 years? And sure, go ahead and get the pizza, you selfish witch. I'll just blow up like a pufferfish and shit for days."

Juliet didn't want this special day with her best friends to be ruined so she said to Marlene, "Go ahead and get the truffle pie, sweetie." To Darryl she said, "Man up and eat the pizza. You don't have Crohn's Disease; you're a hypochondriac."

She had wanted to celebrate her engagement to Paul, show off the beautiful ring he gave her, and talk about her wedding and honeymoon plans. She wanted the day to be about her, for once. But no, Darryl and Marlene always hijacked their get-togethers with their whining and complaining.

"Why do you two have to be so difficult? Just once can't you get along?" Juliet was beginning to think this was a stupid idea. Darryl and Marlene always fought and never got along. Why had she thought today would be any different?

A waiter approached the table. "Ma'am, will there be anyone else joining you today?' There were three place settings but only one guest seated at the table.

"No, we're all here. Let's order, shall we?"

She ordered a pizza in a very gravelly older woman's voice. It sounded like the woman had smoked for decades, even though she looked to be about 35.

After the pizza order was placed, she addressed the waiter in a very deep voice that sounded like a man, "Just keep the damn pizza away from me. I'm allergic to wheat."

Then in a normal voice she apologized to the waiter for the rudeness of her "friends" and ordered two more entrees, a roasted beet salad and a hamburger with extra fries to "share" with the table.

He hurried to the kitchen to enter the order and tell the rest of the waitstaff about the lady at table 8 who ordered three entrees in three different voices. She had even argued with herself about one of the meals.

Marci saw a group of her staff huddled outside the kitchen and whispering among themselves.

MY BEST AND LAST | 81

"You kids don't have enough to do? There's a grill that needs a good scrubbing and a deep freeze to be cleaned out."

Carlo, the waiter, told her about the three orders he had just carried to the table. Just then, a commotion erupted in that direction.

The customer at Table 8 was shouting at a patron at another table. "How dare you insult my Aunt Marlene, you snotty bag of putrescent wind." As Marci reached the table, Juliet was pelting the patron with French fries. Helene, the president of the bank next door to the restaurant, sat in shock as French fries hit her face and ketchup dripped down her Chanel suit.

Marci signaled her staff to call 911 and attempted to calm down Juliet. "Honey, let's just step into my office." Juliet was crying and babbling at this point. "Yes, honey, I know," Marci adopted a soothing tone. "Shhhh, shhhh."

She sent a quick text to her floor manager. TAKE CARE OF HELENE! COMP THE MEAL FOR THE TABLE, GIVE HER A GIFT CARD, AND TELL HER WE WILL BUY HER A NEW SUIT.

"There, there, sweetheart. Tell me what's got you so upset now."

Although Marci wanted to slap some sense into the woman who had caused such a scene in her restaurant, she recognized the signs of mental distress and remained calm. The Decatur PD would be here in a few minutes.

Suddenly, the woman stopped crying and spoke. The timbre of the voice was deep, like a man's.

"Marlene is such a troublemaker. She makes a scene everywhere we go."

Her office intercom squawked, "Um, Ms. King, some uh.... *Friends*.... are here to see you."

"Thank you, Carlo, send them in."

As Juliet was being led away in handcuffs, she turned back to Marci and said in a raspy voice, "Tell your little friend Juliet says 'hello.'"

CHAPTER 19

ACE of SWORDS

The Ace of Swords brings clarity and inspiration to a situation.

CAL

I can tell Laura is miffed with me. She is very short and brusque when she greets me. It is I who should be pissed; I'm the one on trial for murder. I'm beginning to wonder if she is the appropriate attorney for me.

In the center of the conference room table are a high-heeled shoe, a cup, a wine bottle, and a small plastic envelope. Not the ones from the crime scene, obviously. Those are still in police custody. These are props to jog my memory.

"Tell me about Abigail. Did she and Paul marry?"

"I don't think so. After I went…" I hesitated, searching for the right word.

"Berserk?" Laura interjected.

"Yeah. After Abigail filed the restraining order, I backed off. I took a leave of absence and sort of had a breakdown."

"I know. Danny told me."

Why is my attorney conferring with the police detective investigating me?

"He said you spoke about it at the lecture you gave on Saturday."

"I'm not comfortable with you sharing information with the detective who arrested me."

"Let's get one thing straight. I am not sharing any information with Detective Chan. Yes, we have a history and are now friends. I use that friendship to my clients' advantage whenever I can. If you think I have done anything illegal or improprietous, take it to the Bar Association."

She started to gather up her files.

Shit. "Hold on, Laura. I didn't mean to imply you had acted inappropriately."

She laid the files on the table, her eyes still snapping with anger.

"Eagle is tracking Abigail to determine her whereabouts now. What about Juliet? How did she find you?"

"She said a previous client had recommended me. She didn't say who."

"You didn't ask?"

"No."

"And the session on Thursday, that was the first and last one with Juliet?"

"Yes."

Laura sighed. "Why didn't you mention any of these missing items before? Do you not realize how serious this is? Georgia is a death penalty state."

"Things happened so fast after Paul was killed. I was in shock. I didn't think the missing cup was important until I was interrogated."

I realize I had not taken this seriously enough at the outset. "I had assumed because I was innocent that the truth would become obvious, and the real killer would be arrested."

"That hasn't happened. You are the only suspect in Paul's murder. The police have no other suspects. The evidence against you is solid. We must figure out who is framing you. Let's start with Juliet.

"Let's go with the theory that she took the cup at her first session. That's when you noticed it missing. How about the wine? Your fingerprints were on the bottle."

"What type of wine was it?"

"A very expensive one." Laura consults the lab report. "A Chateau Margeaux. 2009."

"Oh. Well, Paul and I bought a bottle of that when we were in France for our second anniversary. We intended to drink it for our tenth anniversary. We never made it to the ten-year mark."

"See if you can find the bottle when you go home, please.

"Now, the shoes. How would she have gotten the shoes?"

Sweet Jesus I don't want to tell her this. "She could have entered my house when I wasn't home. I don't always lock my doors when I take Carl for a walk."

Laura looks at me incredulously.

"I choose to see the best in people."

Evidently Laura does not think this is a virtue. "Look where that has landed you."

For once I did not have a snappy comeback.

Laura hands me a small plastic envelope. "The poison that killed Paul was in an envelope like this."

I turned the envelope over in my hand. Whenever I purchase crystals and rocks, they are usually packaged like... "Wait, that's it! The rock!"

I explained to Laura. "Juliet brought a rock for me to the first session. It was in an envelope like this."

"No other prints but yours are on the bag."

I told Laura about the bandages on Juliet's hands that day.

"You're sure you hadn't met Juliet before that first session?"

"Yes," I said firmly. I hesitated. "There was something vaguely familiar about her, though."

I closed my eyes in concentration.

Laura impatiently tapped the cap of her pen on the table.

I laid my hand on hers. "Do you mind?" I recall the feeling that something was off with Juliet that day, but nothing more.

Laura punches the intercom button. "Sarah, have Marci come in."

Marci walks in with a computer under her arm. The three of us review the video footage of the scene in the restaurant and Marci's office. As soon as I see the woman's face, I exclaim, "That's Juliet!"

"Are you certain?"

"Yes. Absolutely."

Laura punches the intercom button again. "Sarah, have Eagle check out Juliet Morrison." She turns to Marci. "Did the police say where they were taking her?"

"The arresting officer said they were taking her to Summit Ridge."

"Sarah, she's at Summit Ridge. Get Eagle on this right away, please."

Summit Ridge is an inpatient psychiatric facility in Atlanta.

Laura turns back to the video. "It's a shame your security system has no audio. Did she mention Cal by name?"

"No, she just said, 'My little friend.'"

"How long will be she be in Summit Ridge?" Marci asked.

"Three days." Laura and I answer simultaneously. I continue, "They can legally hold her for 72 hours and then they have to release her if she doesn't admit herself for treatment."

Marci was outraged. "She sat in my restaurant and had conversations with two invisible people. That's not grounds to keep her?"

"They'll hold her if she is deemed a danger to herself or others. Otherwise, she will be released. That's the law."

Laura closed the laptop. "We have a potential 'who.' Let's talk about the 'why.' If Juliet killed Paul, why would she frame you?"

"I haven't the slightest idea."

"Did she say anything during your session that was suspicious?"

"She talked about an ex-boyfriend who betrayed her. It reminded me of me and Paul." I had a sudden flash of inspiration. "Could she have been talking about Paul? Maybe she dated Paul? But why would she be upset with me? We've been divorced for a long time."

"None of this makes sense. But I've got Eagle on it. Let's see what she can turn up."

CHAPTER 20

Fear and hopelessness of the Nine of Swords prevent you from seeing reality.

CAL

A few weeks later Laura, Marci, Eagle, and I are in Laura's conference room. Laura is 'tweaking' my defense strategy. She wants to review some new evidence with me.

Eagle pulls a photograph from a manilla folder and slides it across the table to me. "Do you recognize this woman?"

I pick up the photo and wince with recognition. "Of course. It's Abigail, the woman Paul had an affair with."

"Also, the woman who filed a restraining order against you when you bashed in the front windshield of her car." *Gee, thanks, Marce. Got any more nails you want to pound into my coffin?*

Eagle slides a second photograph toward me. "Do you recognize this woman?"

"Yes, that's Juliet Morrison."

"The crazy one!" I press my hand into Marci's knee to silence her. I want to see where this is going.

Laura puts the two photographs side by side. "See here, the space between the eyes, the height of the forehead? You can change a lot of things appearance-wise. Eye color, hair style and color, hairline even. Shape and size of nose and lips, chin and cheek implants, gaps in teeth." She takes a pen and marks the photos, "But there are certain things that don't change, like the shape of the skull and location of the eye sockets.

"It was actually Detective Chan who made this connection. "

"What connection? I don't understand."

Laura sends a text on her phone. The door opens and Detective Chan walks in.

I am enraged. "OH. HELL. NO. Get out. How dare you?" I look at Laura. "What is he doing here?"

"Do you need a valium?" Marci and her valium have been coming to my rescue quite a bit since my arrest.

Definitely, but I ignore her.

My conspiracy theory vibe is pinging. Am I being set up? Are my attorney and her ex-husband, the Detective, part of the plot to frame me? So many crazy things have happened in my life over the last month that I don't think it is beyond the realm of possibility.

"Dr. Cassidy, Cal," Danny Chan puts his hand gently on my arm. "Let me say right off the bat that I do not believe you killed Paul Davis."

I eye him with suspicion. Wouldn't he say that if he and Laura were trying to trick me into confessing?

I pulled my arm away. I am on high alert. I grabbed Marci's hand under the table and squeezed it. She is the only one in the room I trust.

"I understand you don't trust me right now but hear me out. We have cleared all other suspects in Paul's murder except for you."

Marci comes to my defense. "What about Juliet? That woman is bat-shit crazy."

Danny ignores Marci's outburst. "In spite of all the evidence pointing to you, and Detective Bizzell's insistence that you are guilty, I had a gut feeling that you are innocent and are being framed for Paul's murder."

Oh, this guy is good. Buttering me up to get me to trust him and then, boom! He'll pounce on me and send me away for life. With my attorney's help.

"When Laura came to me with the information about Juliet, the missing cup, and the scene at Serendipity, I did some digging into her background. My IT guys could not find any evidence of her existence prior to 2019. Eagle investigated Abigail Stewart. There is no trace of Abigail after 2019.

"On a hunch I asked our guys and Eagle to run both photographs through their facial recognition software. They both came to the same conclusion. Juliet is Abigail."

"How did you even think to compare their photographs? They don't look anything alike."

No one said a word.

I look at Eagle. She is studying an interesting cuticle on her thumb. Laura has an indecipherable look on her face. Detective Chan looked defiant.

"Detective Chan? Why did you compare the photographs?"

"As part of the prosecutorial process, I interviewed your clients. Juliet is the only one that had some inconsistencies in her statements. In conjunction with her erratic behavior at the restaurant, and her message to you, I had enough to warrant further investigation into her."

"You interviewed my clients? How dare you!" I stand up and pace around the room. "My clients have been to hell and back. They have been abused, usually by more than one person—parents, priests, lovers, husbands. My god, one of them was even raped by a policeman."

I look at Laura. "Did you know about this?" I don't wait for an answer.

"Do you know what you have done to these women? Their self-esteem is already in the gutter. It takes me at least six months of steady work to earn their trust. I'm just beginning to see a little chink of light in the souls of some of these women. You just destroyed everything I stand for. Everything I worked for. They will never trust me again."

"Are you finished?" Laura's voice has no hint of remorse.

"No." I shake my finger at both Laura and Danny. "You crossed the line. You went behind my back and messed with my life, my reputation, my work, and the lives of women I care about."

"I'm investigating a murder, Cal. I don't need your permission to interview anyone in connection with you. All your clients and colleagues were more than willing to speak on your behalf. Everyone defended you. They hold you in the highest regard.

"The only exception was Juliet. She dropped not-so-subtle hints about your emotional instability, your infatuation with Paul and his new wife, and your history of violence with Paul's previous lover. She mentioned some details about the restraining order and the divorce that weren't public record. When I asked her how she knew about it she became very combative and defensive.

"Then suddenly, she flipped a switch and reverted to being saccharin sweet, apologizing for sharing those things about you. She assured me you couldn't have killed Paul because you were with her that night. She was your alibi for the night Paul was killed."

"This is the craziest thing I've ever heard. I don't have an alibi for that night. I was home alone working."

"Juliet claims you spent the night together."

"I don't know why she would say that. Wait a minute—like as in—sleeping together?"

My mind is going in a thousand directions at once. I am trying to pull all these tangled threads together and make sense of this madness. I can't.

I look at Marci. "I'll take that valium now."

CHAPTER 21

The Three of Pentacles represents teamwork and collaboration.

DANNY

Laura had warned me that Cal would explode when she found out I had interviewed her clients. It's obvious she doesn't trust me yet. I can't blame her for that.

I could tell Cal was still confused by the information we were throwing at her. I'll give her credit; she was handling it well.

"I interviewed the admitting psychiatrist at Summit Ridge. Juliet exhibits signs of Dissociative Identity Disorder. He believes when she had the mental break, possibly over the failed romance with Paul, the other personalities emerged. He identified at least three other personalities.

"My theory is at least one of those personalities decided to kill Paul and frame you for it. How long did Abigail and Paul stay together?"

"I have no idea. It couldn't have been long, though, because Paul married Irina about six months after our divorce was finalized."

"Are you saying now that Abigail or Juliet is a suspect that Cal is off the hook for Paul's murder?"

"Not really, Marci." I lay my hand on top of Marci and Cal's clasped hands. I feel Cal tense and her hand jerks. But she doesn't move it away.

"We can't prove any of this. There is no evidence that Juliet killed Paul. All the evidence, physical and circumstantial, points to Cal. Juliet covered her tracks well.

Cal is sitting very still with her eyes closed. She speaks after a few minutes. "I need to lay this all out, get it organized, so I can deal with it.

"We know that Juliet had the opportunity to steal a cup with my fingerprints on it on the day of her appointment.

"She probably stole the bottle of wine that day, too. She couldn't have taken the shoes then because I went upstairs to my closet to get the lavender oil for her burned fingers. It took me a while to find it; I left her alone for at least five minutes. She had to have stolen the shoes before her appointment."

"How would she have entered your home?" I saw Laura grimace and shake her head.

"There are times that I take Carl for a walk or run back over to my office in the Psych building for a short while, without locking my door."

"You *what*?" If that sounded judgmental, it was.

"I told her she was too trusting," said Marci.

Cal was irritated. "I lock my door now. Don't make a big deal of it."

Laura spoke up. "It is a big deal, Cal. One that could get you convicted if we can't connect Juliet to this crime with some real evidence."

"How can we find some evidence? Or get Juliet to confess?" Cal looks around the room at us. I wonder if she realizes how naïve she sounds.

I'm not about to tell her that the only way I have thought of so far puts her in grave danger of being killed herself.

CHAPTER 22

The gift of love is presented to you in the Ace of Cups.

CAL

"How can I prove my innocence?" No one answers me.

"It's not a rhetorical question, people. I want an answer." I look at Laura, Eagle, and Danny. Their faces are blank.

"Okay, I'm done." I push my chair back from the conference room table. "If you'll excuse me, I'm going home to process this."

"I'm coming with you," says Marci. "You don't need to be alone."

"Actually, I do need to be alone. I am mentally, physically, and emotionally exhausted and I need to regroup." I give Marci a kiss on the cheek. "I'll call you later."

I am shaken by the revelations of the last two hours. Unsteady on my feet, I stumble as I walk down the steps of Laura's law firm. Thankfully, someone is behind me and catches me as I fall.

"Hey, let me give you a ride home."

It's Danny. Laura's office is just a few blocks from my house, an easy stroll, but I am too tired to protest.

He opens the front passenger door to the police cruiser and helps me into the car. We are silent during the five-minute drive. Turning into my driveway, I laugh. "I like riding in the front seat of a police car much better than riding in the cage." I gesture to the back seat.

"Yeah, sorry about that. We didn't really have a choice. That's standard procedure."

He turns off the ignition and says, "Stay right there. Let me help you into the house."

"I'm not an invalid. I'm just tired." When he opens the door and I exit the car, I step on his foot and lose my balance. I banged the top of my head into his chin. Having nothing else to lean on, I lean into him to steady myself.

I feel him shudder and I sense I have invaded his space. I pull away, my back against the car. "Sorry about that. Now you know my secret. I'm an absolute klutz."

"Oh, I noticed you were a klutz when you laughed yourself out of your chair when I first met you."

He takes a step forward and puts his arm around me for support.

I feel my heart flutter in my chest. *Oh my God, I have not been this close to a man in years.*

We stand there for a minute, neither of us moving. I take in the warmth of his body and subtle scent of his cologne. Closing my eyes, I lift my face to the light of the sun peeking through the pine trees that surround my cottage. I feel calm and peace returning.

I open my eyes at the exact moment this man who interrogated me, arrested me, and had me indicted for murder, kisses me.

He kisses me lightly at first, as if waiting for my response. Before I can check myself, I move into him. I have never been kissed so deeply and passionately. I've been waiting all my life for a kiss like this.

Holy freaking Mother of God I think my underpants are on fire.

Crap! Did I say that out loud?

Danny laughs and presses his body against mine.

"Doc, my pants are on fire, too."

This is getting crazier by the minute.

CHAPTER 23

The Two of Cups symbolizes mutual respect and attraction.

DANNY

Dammit. All that 'impeccable integrity' my therapist friend says I have just disintegrated.

Dear God, what a kiss.

The spell is broken when Cal pushes me away. "No! One minute you are trying to put me in jail and the next you're making a move on me."

I release the embrace and step back, mentally chastising myself. "Dr. Cassidy, I apologize. I don't know what came over me. That was totally inappropriate."

Cal is wiping her mouth like she is trying to erase the kiss.

"My life has been in turmoil since Paul's death. The college put me on leave until the trial is over. People that

I've known for decades are avoiding me. My reputation is in tatters and my life's work is destroyed.

"Then I find out a client of mine, who is Paul's crazy ex-girlfriend, killed him and framed me. I'm trying my damnedest to keep it together and stayed grounded."

"I'm sorry. I didn't mean to complicate things for you."

"You 'complicated' things for me the day I met you."

"How did I do that? I am doing my job."

"You kiss all your murder suspects?"

"I apologized for that. I was out of line."

"Don't beat yourself up. You didn't get your signals crossed."

What the hell is this woman trying to say?

"Neither of us need this kind of complication or distraction in our personal or our professional lives."

"I'm not sure I understand your point."

"My point is, Detective, the attraction is mutual."

Everything in me is saying, "Leave now."

"Would you like to come in for a cup a coffee, Detective?"

"I would love to, Doctor. Got any sugar?" So much for listening to the voice of reason.

CHAPTER 24

A new relationship is taking shape in the Page of Pentacles. However new beginnings can often be unstable.

CAL

We make coffee together, moving in tandem around my kitchen like an old married couple. I protest when Danny pours my coffee and adds cream. Not that I'm a control freak or anything…

He hands me a cup and I take a cautious sip. The coffee is perfect. The woo-woo side of me wants to take this as a sign that this man is my perfect match. My skeptical side says, "do you really want to set yourself up for another broken heart?"

Cal, The Psychologist, counsels, "This is interesting. Let's see where it goes."

It occurs to me I have as many voices inside my head as Juliet does.

We carry our cups to the living room and sit on either end of the sofa. Carl settles himself comfortably between us. Sometimes Carl is the wisest one in the room. "Keep your distance, humans," he seems to be saying.

I'm extremely nervous, and I can tell Danny is as well. He makes small talk. "Every woman I've ever known has tons of these blanket things. What's with that?"

Without a word, I tossed a chenille throw to him. I get up, arrange a few soft pillows under his elbows, and motion for him to put his feet on the coffee table. He looks at me in amusement. Until I tuck the throw around him and he burrows into the soft cave I created for him. "Oh, yeah, now I get it."

Carl lays his head in Danny's lap.

Traitor.

Neither of us know what to say so we sit for a while in silence, enjoying our coffee.

What the hell am I doing? Men say they like my independent streak at first but when they start to feel a little bit threatened, they flex their macho muscle. Once a man begins to tell me what to do, where to do it, how to do it, why to do it…well, let's just say my anger management issues show up. I have never had a relationship that didn't end badly.

Why did I invite him in for coffee? Why didn't I just send him away?

Oh yeah, the kiss.

Dear God, what a kiss.

Danny clears his throat. "Why did you decide to become a psychologist?"

My guard goes up. He doesn't need to hear about my abusive mother and absent father and all the reasons I went into psychology to try to fix myself. For all I know he'd use it against me in trial.

I give him the G rated version. "I had an eighth-grade teacher who took an interest in me. You know how tough middle school can be, especially for a gawky, nerdy kid. She helped me understand my value and my worth. When I graduated from high school, Mrs. Ferrin and her husband gave me a scholarship to the University of Georgia. All four years were paid for by a schoolteacher and her janitor husband. Those two guardian angels changed the course of my life. They helped me discover my life's purpose—to help people like they helped me."

"I can't imagine you were ever gawky or nerdy."

I pull a photo album off a built-in bookcase and turn a few pages. "See?"

I can see him struggling not to laugh. He doesn't know what to say. I was all cat-eye glasses, braces, crooked bangs, and mismatched knee socks.

"To my credit, in tenth grade, the braces came off, I got contact lenses, and Mrs. Ferrin took me to a beauty salon for my first professional haircut." I turned the page and showed him another photograph. The transformation was remarkable. That was the year I was voted Junior Homecoming Queen.

He turned back to the first page. "I don't know...I kind of dig those knee socks and braces."

Dammit, this man has all the right moves.

It is time for him to go.

"I decided to become a police officer for the same reason—to help people. Want to hear about it?"

It would be rude of me to say, "no."

"I'd love to."

CHAPTER 25

The Two of Wands signifies a new relationship filled with passion!

DANNY

"I grew up in a not-so-great area of Atlanta. My parents had a dry-cleaning business on Hill Street. Back in the 60s there were a lot of race riots and some drugs—not like it is now, of course, and some gang activity, too.

"I was the only Asian kid in the neighborhood, and I didn't fit in anywhere. There was this one policeman who took an interest in me. He kept an eye on our dry-cleaning business after my dad died. He was a good man, a good cop, and I decided I wanted to be like him and make a difference in people's lives when I grew up."

"And have you? Made a difference in people's lives?"

"I think so. I hope so. For the first 10 years I was on the force, the Hill Street area was my beat. I knew all the families—their children, the grandparents. I got a couple of churches to start after-school programs for the kids so they weren't roaming the streets and getting into trouble. Then they started day care programs, and one even offered vocational training. I think it made a difference in a lot of people's lives."

Cal's voice is soft. "It sounds like *you* made the difference. There is a quote I love, 'Those who are crazy enough to think they can change the world are the ones who do it.'"

My hand is resting on the dog between us. Cal reaches over and places her hand on top of mine. I wonder if she feels the little shiver of excitement I feel when she touches me.

"Do you mind if I make more coffee? Can I get you some, too?"

She hands me her cup. "Two scoops. And half coffee, half...." I hold up my hand. "I know. I pay attention."

While I'm in the kitchen waiting for the coffee to brew, I hear her whisper to Carl, "I think I'm in trouble, buddy."

The last time I felt this way was when I was fifteen and the girl I liked agreed to go out on a date with me.

"This woman likes me," I thought.

My next thought was, "I'm a dead man if Biz finds out."

CHAPTER 26

The Four of Cups asks you to leave the past behind and move forward with a new romance.

DANNY

I hand Cal her coffee. She takes a sip and smiles. "Kudos," she says. "You really do pay attention." I'm sure it was a coincidence, but under the blanket I hear the dog snort.

Cal pats his back. "He does that a lot when he's dreaming. And he snores like a freight train. That's why he sleeps on the porch, weather permitting."

The sun is setting and fireflies are beginning to flicker around the trees in the front yard. "Why don't we go sit on the porch? It's a beautiful evening." We settled into two antique rocking chairs.

Cal's bungalow reminds me of my cabin. Nothing ostentatious about it, just simple and functional. "This is a great little house. How did you find it?"

"It belongs to the college. It was where the Dean lived in the 1930s. I stumbled upon it about twelve years ago. It had been abandoned for decades and slated for demolition to make room for a parking lot for the museum."

Through the trees I could make out the corner of the Anthropology Museum in the distance.

"It was in horrible shape. The porch had holes in it and racoons had built nests underneath. The windows were broken out and the door was half off the hinges. It looked like it was a hangout for vagrants at one time, but it was completely abandoned by the time I saw it."

I looked around the porch. The wide oak plank floorboards and railings had been carefully restored and were in pristine condition.

I'm not sure why but she was watching me closely.

Cal spoke cautiously. "You may think this is weird, but as soon as I saw this place, I experienced something akin to déjà vu. I had this overwhelming sense of 'home.' I don't think I found the cottage. I think it found me."

Laura had mentioned there was a facet of her new client that puzzled her. "She is well-educated, an M.D. and a psychologist. Yet, she has a spiritual side that makes her sound like a nut at times."

At the time I was still investigating Cal for Paul's murder, so I questioned Laura about it. "Spiritual side like Protestant, Catholic, or Jewish?"

"Oh no, nothing normal. She reads tarot cards, believes crystals have magical powers, and talks to angels."

Ahhhh, that's why Cal is observing my reactions. For a brief moment, I hope she can't read my mind. My thoughts about this woman would make a hooker blush.

CHAPTER 27

The Magician is a card of manifestation. You have everything needed to make your dreams come true.

CAL

I'm watching Danny closely to see how he reacts to what Marci calls my "woo-woo" side. Laura jokes that I put the "psycho" in "psychologist" but I'm not paying her for her opinion. I'm paying her to keep me out of the electric chair.

I'm curious as to what Danny's reaction will be. I decided to go all in. "I think the cottage is haunted."

"Really?" is all Danny says. Not much for me to go on.

"Yes. Sometimes I feel a weird "other-worldly" presence in the house. Like someone is sitting right beside me on the sofa. Once, I woke up in the middle of the night and saw a young woman dressed in the fashion of the 30s or 40sat the foot of my bed. As I reached to turn on the light, I heard her say, 'Beware.' And then she was gone."

"'Beware'? That's weird."

"It was the night before Juliet's first session. Do you believe in the afterlife, Danny?"

"I honestly have to say I have never given ghosts or the afterlife much thought. Although I did have something strange happen once. When I was a rookie cop, my TO and I responded to a horrible single car accident near an old church cemetery.

"The driver had lost control of the car and hit a tree. He was hurt pretty badly, and we had to pry him out. As the EMTs were loading him into the ambulance he asked about the little girl.

"I panicked, thinking there was a child trapped in the car. But he said, 'No, she wasn't in the car.' She had walked out from behind a tombstone, climbed into the car, and held his hand until we got there. She told him her name was Amelia. He said, 'She told me I would be OK and that I had a lot of good things to do before I died.'"

"I went back to that cemetery later and looked around. Near where his car had crashed was a tombstone with the name, "Amelia Anderson. Born 1902. Died 1909."

He smiled at me. "That's my only ghost story."

I'm curious. "What's your explanation for that?"

Danny laughed. "Cal, I do my best to keep people safe and alive. I leave the dead people to...."

I interrupt. "Nut? Quacks? Charlatans?"

"I was going to say the coroner."

CHAPTER 28

Conflict is a part of every relationship. The Nine of Swords reminds us that communication is the key.

DANNY

It's getting late but I don't want to leave. "I'm getting hungry. Would you like to get some dinner?"

Cal yawned. I took the chance to spoof her. "Am I really that boring?"

She laughed. She does not have a girly laugh. She brays like a donkey. For some reason, I like that.

And then she turned serious. Crap.

"Danny, this has been a lovely afternoon," she began.

I held up my hand to stop her. I didn't want to hear the rest. "I understand. You're right. We'd have to sneak around and not let anyone know we were seeing each other."

I headed down the steps to my car.

She didn't stop me. Dammit, she didn't stop me.

CHAPTER 29

The challenge of the Two of Swords is to release your fears of pursuing a new relationship.

CAL

My heart said, "Stop him."
My head said, "Let him go."

CHAPTER 30

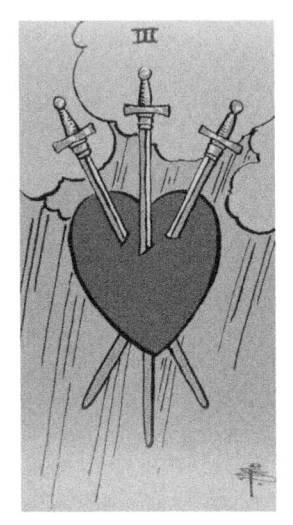

Heartbreak, loss, and separation are weighing on your mind in the Three of Swords.

CAL

I check in with Laura every day. Juliet disappeared as soon as she was released from Summit Ridge. Both Eagle and Danny have attempted to locate her without success. She's a ghost.

My trial is set for September. The charge is capital murder. Unless Juliet can be found and somehow forced to confess, Laura says I am facing a sentence of life in prison. Without parole. She doesn't mention the death penalty, but I know it's a possibility because the media reports say I deserve it for committing such a heinous crime.

I avoid eating at Serendipity because I know Danny eats there often. I don't want to run into him. He acted like a child at my house. Why are men such babies?

If he had let me finish my sentence that day, I was going to say, "This has been a lovely afternoon and I'd love to spend the evening with you." Against my best judgment, I meant The. Whole. Evening.

But he overreacted and left in a huff.

"I'm sorry, honey," said Marci when I called her that night.

"I really thought I had met a man who was different. Looks like I dodged a bullet."

Since I was still on leave from the college until after the trial, I spent the majority of my time working on a new book, *Zzzzzingle!* It is about the freedom and joie de vivre that single women find in the second half of life.

I would never admit it, but I feel like a fraud writing it.

One, my life is void of joie de vivre. I am under indictment and mooning over the man who arrested me. No joy there.

Two, my literal freedom is in jeopardy. Without a miracle, I'll be behind bars before long.

Three, I am not able to travel to promote my books. A condition of my bail is that I do not leave Georgia. Anyway, my publisher says no one wants to come to a lecture or a book signing by 'the self-help guru murderess.'

I've seen some snarky articles about me online. I used to read them all, but people are really vicious. I process things with Jim once a week under the guise of "catching up" but it's really therapy. He, Gwen, and Marci are the tribe that keeps me sane. Marci comes over as often as she can, but summer is her busy season at the restaurant.

I went shopping at my favorite boutique in Decatur a month ago and saw Irina Davis, Paul's widow. When she saw me, she froze, and then started yelling in Russian and pointing at me. The boutique owner asked me to leave. I have become a pariah in my hometown.

CHAPTER 31

The King of Cups embodies the energy of compassion and empathy.

DANNY

Once a case is solved and a trial date is set, I don't have anything to do with it until it is time for trial prep by the prosecution. In theory, I should not have the file for the Davis murder still on my desk.

I keep it hidden from Biz in my top desk drawer.

I have to use Eagle Finegan for any investigation and follow up I can't do. Biz found out I had asked our IT department to put a trace on Juliet Morrison after she was discharged from the psych hospital. She was furious. She created such a ruckus in the squad room that the unit commander pulled me aside and asked what was going on.

"It's just Biz being Biz, Captain. You know how she gets when she doesn't get her way. Don't mention it to her; I'll smooth it over."

I hated throwing Biz under the bus, but she was out of line reacting that way. We had never disagreed before now to this extent. There is a growing chasm between us. We stopped eating at Serendipity together or having a drink after shifts.

I still eat at Serendipity every day. Marci is not as friendly as she used to be. I understand. She and Cal have been best friends since childhood.

Today, I worked up the courage to ask her about Cal. I haven't seen her since that day in May.

Marci pulls up a chair. "I'm worried about her. She's become a recluse. Have you read some of the stuff about her in the newspaper and online?"

I have. There are some very sick people out there. "Did she tell you about the last time I saw her?"

Marci looks uncomfortable. "Yes."

"Can I be honest with you, Marci? You've known me a long time and I think you know what kind of person I am."

Marci didn't say anything.

"This is confidential. I'm working with Eagle to locate Juliet. I have a plan to get Juliet to confess."

CHAPTER 32

The Strength card reminds us we can overcome both internal and external struggles.

CAL

Marci called as I was taking Carl for his last walk of the evening. I assured her my doors were locked. I had even had my locks changed when Laura suggested that Juliet might have copied the key taped to the underside of my outdoor rocking chair. "Perhaps that is how she made calls from your office to Paul's house." That call log had baffled me. This seemed a reasonable explanation.

"Let's go to the lake and watch fireworks tomorrow night. Just me and you, like old times."

"Lake Lanier is too far. And Fourth of July is so crowded up there. Let's stay home and watch fireworks on TV."

"Not Lanier. Let's go to this little lake in Roswell. There's this cute little community called Mountain Park. One of my customers lives there."

"I'll go if you make curried chicken salad and homemade croissants. And cream cheese brownies." Marci knows the way to my heart is gastronomical.

"You got it. I'll pick you up at 7:00."

The next evening, she picked me up at seven on the dot. The brownies smelled wonderful, and I ate one in the car.

We made small talk, chatting about the progress of my book (dismal) and the price of tomatoes at the Farmer's Market (exorbitant). I have missed hanging out with Marci.

"Who is the customer in Mountain Park? Do I know them?"

"Oh my gosh, did you see that car turn right in front of me without a blinker." I hadn't. I was busy foraging for another cream cheese brownie.

We turned off Hwy 92 onto a side road. "So, who is this customer?"

"Look at that deer! Oh, you missed it. It was so cute!"

"Why are you acting so weird?"

We pulled into the driveway of a small cabin that had a view of the lake. I assumed we'd have a front row seat for the fireworks shortly. Marci unloaded the food onto the patio table in the front yard. Then she got back into the car. "I forgot the wine. I'll be right back."

What the hell? I yelled it aloud as her car retreated down the dirt road. "What the hell, Marci?"

I was furious when Danny walked out the front door of the cabin.

CHAPTER 33

QUEEN of SWORDS

The Queen of Swords takes a logical approach and makes decisions based on facts.

DANNY

Cal didn't say a word when she saw me, but I have never seen anyone—man, woman, or beast—as enraged as she was. Her face turned all kinds of shades of red and purple.

She sat down at the picnic table and closed her eyes. She didn't speak for a few minutes. When she looked up, she smiled at me. It was not a nice smile.

"Hello, Danny."

Her face had returned to its natural color. "You have a lovely little place," she said sweetly. "Does Uber pick up here?"

"You seem pretty angry with me and Marci."

Cal shrugged. "Marci and I have been through a lot together. We'll get over it."

"How about us?"

"Doubtful." She shook her head. "Marci drove away with my purse in the car. Would you please call an Uber for me?"

I sat in a chair beside Cal. She moved her chair away from me.

"I apologize for the way I acted at your house. My pride was wounded. I don't take rejection well."

"Oh, you're psychic? You knew that I was going to reject you?"

"It seemed obvious."

"Actually, Danny, your fear was ungrounded. I had planned to ask you to stay the night. Now I'm glad I didn't. It's obvious a relationship between us would not work out."

"So, now *you're* psychic? Why wouldn't a relationship between us work out?"

"Danny, I'm not some young girl you can mold and manipulate into the kind of woman you want and need. I am a mature, independent woman who does not need a man to complete me."

"Whoa. What's that all about?"

"All men your age want a trophy girlfriend. You prefer beauty over brains."

"That's an unfair assessment of me. Mind telling me what's gotten into you?"

"Please just call an Uber."

I open the app and schedule an Uber. "They are an hour forty-five out, Cal. It's July 4th."

"Fine. I can wait."

She opened the picnic basket and fixed herself a plate. The food smelled terrific. I dished up a large helping for myself.

"This is amazing. Did you make this?"

"No. Marci."

I sighed. It was going to be a very long wait for Uber.

"You and Marci are lucky to have each other. My best friend is very angry with me right now."

I saw Cal hesitate, and then keep eating.

"Yeah, Biz is furious because I don't believe you're guilty."

I glance at Cal out of the corner of my eye. I can tell she is listening. "When she found out I asked the IT department to track Juliet, she was livid. I've had to ask Eagle to continue investigating on the side. I think she's close to finding Juliet. She has a few leads."

Cal stopped eating and faced me. "Why would you do that? Help me, I mean."

"I told you. I believe you are innocent."

"Why?"

"During the interrogation, when Biz threw that photograph of Paul on the table, you recoiled in horror. You didn't fake that reaction. Therefore, I concluded you were not the murderer."

"What if I had paid someone to do it?"

"I thought of that. Your bank account didn't show any unaccounted-for payments. None of your friends or colleagues acted suspiciously when we interviewed them. There was no chatter on the street about someone hiring a contract killer to kill Paul."

Cal looked uncomfortable. "You went through my life with a fine-toothed comb."

"Yes, we did."

Cal was silent for a minute, then, a genuine smile played across her face. "Thank you, Danny."

I have an inkling that a heretofore impenetrable wall is starting to crumble.

CHAPTER 34

The Lovers desire for passion is tempered by trust and respect.

CAL

I have seriously underestimated Danny Chan. "I'm sorry I've judged you so harshly. Maybe I was judging myself, too, for how I felt about you."

"Felt? Past tense?"

"I might reconsider."

"Under what conditions?"

"Let's start with another kiss."

Was it a sign from the Universe that just as our lips touched, the fireworks started on the dock below us?

I had his shirt unbuttoned and halfway off by the time we stumbled through his front door. He unzipped my sundress and I try my best to sexy-shimmy out of it.

"STOP!"

I freeze mid-shimmy. Just as well: the Spanx is glued to my body, and I am having little success peeling it off my sweaty skin.

I knew it. I freaking knew it. Middle aged men can't handle a middle-aged woman's body.

I lean over and yank on my dress to pull it up. It is twisted around my ankles. I suck in my stomach; my muffin top is spilling over the Spanx. I'm too angry to care about it or the cellulite on my thighs.

I lose my balance. Danny catches me and props me against the wall.

"Cal, stand still. If you try to walk with that dress around your ankles, you'll fall and break your neck. You've got me so worked up I'd probably have sex with you first and then call the coroner."

Oh.

Why do I always think the worst about myself and other people?

I stand still while he kneels to help me out of the dress. He is completely confused by the Spanx so I jerk it off as quickly as I can. I desperately want to neatly fold the dress, but I forget about neatness and folding altogether when Danny remains kneeling and pulls me to him. His finger traces the outline of my panties, and his mouth is hot against me. I am moaning with anticipation. Suddenly he stops.

He stands up, a sheepish grin on his face. "I'm old. Can we do this in bed? My knees are killing me."

He pulls me through the door of his bedroom.

The first time was passionate and wild. We couldn't get enough of each other. Afterward, we lay entwined in each other's arms, feeling the headiness of physical satisfaction.

The second time was slow and delicious. We pace ourselves, tracing body parts with our tongues, exploring other body parts with our fingers. When he brought me to climax with his tongue and fingers, I writhed with pleasure so deep and complete that I felt momentarily paralyzed.

The third time.... I'd heard about transcendental sex before. I can only describe it as a meeting of souls that was sacred.

"I love you."

Who said that? Did I say it? Did he say it?

I realize it was Danny, half-singing, half humming, Nat King Cole's song, "I love you, for sentimental reasons." He spoons me close and kisses my neck. "Don't go home tonight."

I am exhausted, half-paralyzed, and sex drunk. "No car. Must stay."

CHAPTER 35

*A new level of satisfaction and intimacy
is achieved with the Nine of Cups.*

CAL

Early the next morning, before daylight, his phone rang. We both stir. He looks at it, then turns it off.

I feel a knee nudged between my legs. A minute later, my legs seem to be located somewhere over my head but having been up half the night wallowing in hedonistic pleasures and not yet having had coffee, I can't be sure.

My body responds to his touch like a taut violin string humming with desire. Then, the unexpected happens. Something I had never experienced. We came at the same time.

My heart is bursting with love and longing. Twin Souls, indeed.

I am done for. "I need coffee, but I can't move."

He pushes back the covers and gets out of bed, then tucks the sheet and quilt around my shoulders. "Stay here and stay warm. I'll be back in a minute with coffee." He stops me before I can speak. "I know…two scoops per cup."

Ten minutes later he puts a steaming mug in my hand and a chenille throw around my shoulders. I rake my fingers through my hair in an attempt to smooth it. He reaches over and brushes my unruly bedhead bangs out of my eyes. "You are so beautiful to me." His kisses taste like sex and coffee.

"How very Joe Cocker of you. But you must not have your contacts in."

Danny laughs. "You know, for a shrink I would think you'd have that whole 'self-esteem thing' mastered.

I take a sip of coffee. "Self-esteem has nothing to do with bedhead, morning breath, and crusty sleep eyes."

"Haven't you ever heard that beauty is in the eye of the beholder?"

"I think your 'eye' is just a mite clouded by all those orgasms you had last night and this morning."

Danny takes my hand. "About last night…." His voice trails off.

I'm suddenly wary. Is this where he says, "Don't call me, I'll call you."?

"I don't even have the words to describe how amazing last night was. I wanted our first time together to be a romantic experience you'd never forget—something sweet and gentle. And it was…and then it was wild…and then it was…spiritual." Danny cups my face in his hands.

"You are the most intriguing and mesmerizing and sexy woman I've ever met. Where have you been all my life?"

Is this guy for real? I make a mental note in case I ever write a romance novel instead of self-help books.

"I've been right here all along. We could have been at Serendipity at the same time hundreds of times over the years and just never noticed each other. Wouldn't it be crazy if the Universe had to orchestrate my arrest for us to find each other?"

Danny shook his head. "I can think of a million better ways for us to have met. Listen, seriously, we have to talk about what comes next."

Reality sets in. "I guess the trial comes next."

"No, you can't go to trial. It will be brutal."

"I keep hoping Laura will figure something out or Eagle will find Juliet, or you'll find a new clue. Something to prove my innocence. Do you know how hard this has been to have my reputation sullied, to be shunned by friends and some of my colleagues? My life has blown up."

Danny takes me in his arms. "No, I don't. I can only imagine what you are going through. You told me once that I am a complication in your life. If a relationship between us is too much for you with everything else you are facing, we can put this on hold."

I playfully grabbed his hand. "Don't go anywhere. You and Marci are my lifelines. I need your help to get through this."

"I told Marci yesterday that Eagle is close to locating Juliet. When we find her, I have a plan to get a confession.

"In the meantime, though, Biz is still convinced you are guilty. I can't budge her on the evidence."

"She's jealous."

"She's married. She's not jealous."

"You're her best friend, right?" Danny nods. "How long have you been partners?"

"Almost fifteen years."

"She just doesn't want things to change between you. I'm a threat to a shift in her world."

As if on cue, Danny's phone vibrates on the nightstand. "Hold on, it's Biz again."

"Hey Biz, what's up." He listens for a moment. I can hear the yak yak yak of Danny's partner on the other end of the phone. "Yeah, no, I'm not at home. I'm having breakfast. What? Pancakes and bacon. Why? No, no don't meet me. I'll be at the station in 30 minutes. No, really, I'm just leaving now." I hear more yakking.

Danny ends the call. "We must be very careful. My pension is on the line if anyone finds out we are seeing each other."

"I'll swear Marci to secrecy."

"Good. This is serious. You are still under indictment and awaiting trial. The arresting officer and the suspect…it will be a nightmare for both of us if anyone finds out."

"What about Laura?" A thought occurs to me. "What *about* Laura—you and she were once married? I can't picture you two together."

"It was a long time ago. And a long story I will tell you some other time. I need to get going and meet Biz. I'll drop you at your house on the way. Let's keep Laura out of it for now."

In the shower it was difficult to keep our hands off each other. We were still basking in the new-relationship-post-sex glow.

Danny dressed quickly and I threw on my sundress and sandals. "There is so much more we need to talk about. We can't meet at your house or my condo. I think we'll be safe meeting here. How about seven tonight?"

"I'll check my calendar. My company is in great demand. So many meetings and social events, you know."

Danny kissed me lightly. "I'm glad you haven't lost your sense of humor. It will be OK, Cal. I don't yet know how, but it will be."

CHAPTER 36

The Five of Wands shows up when clashing egos create conflict and disagreement.

DANNY

I'm gathering up my wallet and keys in the bedroom when I hear the front door open.

"What the hell is going on here?"

I know that voice all too well.

Cal is standing in the open doorway.

Biz is on my front porch. She is madder than a nest of hornets.

"Unbelievable," is all she says.

Cal starts to speak but I touch her arm. "I don't mean to pull rank but let me handle this."

"Biz, I am taking Cal home. I'll meet you at the precinct in 30 minutes."

Biz stomps off my porch, slams her car door, and slings gravel as she speeds out of my driveway.

On the drive to her house, Cal asks, "How bad is it?"

"If she reports me, it's over. I'll be fired. I'm hoping she will listen to reason and not interfere."

Cal reaches over the console, placing her hand on my leg. "Maybe this isn't the right time for us, or maybe it's just not right."

I pull off the road and into the first parking lot I see. I put the car in park and face Cal. "This is worth the risk. If I lose everything in my life, but still have you, then I've lost nothing."

My words bring tears to her eyes. "It took me a long time to find you. I'm not letting you go."

For the rest of the ride, we were silent.

I've been married twice and only now, with Cal, do I understand what love really means.

CHAPTER 37

A choice is presented by the Two of Wands: a partner appears to take your plans to the next level.

DANNY

I drop Cal at her house and head over to the precinct.

It is much more serious than I let on to Cal. I saw Biz's face when she stood at my door. Her fists were clenched. I could see her trembling, doing her best to maintain control and not strangle Cal.

She couldn't mask the pain and shock of betrayal. I read her eyes, "How could you do this with a suspect? How could you do this to *me*?"

I know Biz as well as I know myself. She will double down with the conviction that Cal is guilty. Cal is as good as dead. Biz will see to it that the prosecutor seeks the death penalty.

Eagle is waiting for me outside. "I found Juliet." She hands me a file.

I don't open it. I have bigger fish to fry with Biz.

As soon as I entered the squad room, Captain Kim waved me over. "What is up with Biz? She came in here slamming doors and drawers and anything else she could find. She's waiting for you in the conference room."

She is seated at the table. She is drinking a cup of coffee and there is one on the table across from her. I sit and pick up the cup.

"Poisoned?"

She doesn't crack a smile.

"How could you, Danno? Do you know what you are risking?" Her voice gets louder. "Do you understand what you are asking me to do? Betray my oath, put aside everything I stand for, just to humor some crazy midlife crisis of yours?" She is gesturing wildly. I check to make certain the cameras and microphone in the room are off.

"I'm asking you to trust me and listen to me. Please."

"Trust you? Oh, that's rich. How about you trust me? Trust the evidence, pal, that Caroline Cassidy is guilty as hell."

"Do you remember one of our first cases together—the lawyer who was accused of killing his law partner? Everybody, me included, thought he was guilty."

Biz's brow furrowed. It was not a pleasant memory. Jerry Levinson proclaimed his innocence until the day he was shanked in federal prison and died.

Biz had a hunch, a feeling, that he was innocent. "There's more to this than meets the eye," she had told me repeatedly.

All the evidence pointed to Jerry's guilt. Physical evidence at the crime scene: the gas can with Jerry's fingerprints on it, in the burned-out house where the partner's charred body was found. A life insurance policy taken out four months earlier with Jerry as the beneficiary.

The files that mysteriously appeared, indicating the partner had uncovered some shady transactions by Levinson.

"You believed in his innocence, and you asked me to trust you. And I did."

"Even after Jerry was convicted, we kept the case open. One day you found an anomaly in the DNA report. Something in the lab report didn't match the partner's medical records."

Biz was listening. I sensed her softening.

"Then a guy was arrested in Costa Rica on a drug charge, and it came to light it was the partner living there under a false identity. He had faked his death and framed Jerry for it. He was responsible for the shady dealings, not Jerry, and he did all that to cover it up."

"Jerry had died two months prior. We uncovered the truth too late."

"I have the same confidence in Cal's innocence that you did with Jerry's. Let's not be too late with the truth for Cal."

CHAPTER 38

Friendship takes center stage and lifts your spirits with the Three of Cups.

CAL

Carl jumped on me as soon as I opened the door to my cottage. "I'll bet you are starving, big boy. I didn't expect to be gone all night." I fed and watered him and then we sat together on the front porch, enjoying the cool morning air. Atlanta is brutishly hot during the summer, but mornings can be pleasant under the canopy of the pines in my yard.

I don't even know what to think about last night.

Three months ago, I was very content with my single life. I didn't date and was happy to teach and write books and spend time with friends. I had created a simple but fulfilling life that I loved.

Everything about that life I so carefully created was now a shambles. Especially my resolve to remain single for the rest of my life.

Marci barreled into my driveway. "Well?" she yelled, hanging halfway out of the car door.

I motioned for her to join me on the porch.

"I drove by your house last night around 1:00 a.m. and then at 6:00 a.m. I know you weren't home." She looked at me expectantly. "Tell me everything. Do not leave out any juicy details."

"Not without an apology from you first. You tricked me."

"I had to get you out of your own way. You and Danny are meant to be together."

"Maybe. He has a lot of depth. And kindness. He is a very nice man. I could see myself falling in love with him."

"Falling? Did you say falling? Hmmmpf. Girl, you drove off that cliff at high speed yesterday. You're in a free fall at 90 miles an hour."

This is the first time I have ever held back details from Marci. Whatever is going on between Danny and me feels different and I want to protect it.

I give her the, "I'm still processing it," excuse.

"Oh, I see? That good, huh? Multiple orgasms, I presume?"

I blush.

"I can read you like a book, you know. I respect your boundaries. But I don't have to like them." She looks wistful. "I'm just a little jealous."

I scoot my rocking chair closer to hers. "I know, baby. I know."

We sit for a while, rocking and holding hands. Marci keeps the grief of losing her husband tightly controlled. She told me once that she felt if she let go and let it out, she wouldn't recover. I've never pressed her to open up and process her grief differently. Everyone has their own way of dealing with tragedy.

"Since you set me up with such convincing chicanery, you need to answer a few questions. You've known Danny a lot longer than I have. Have you ever seen him with a date? Why isn't he married? How long has he been divorced?"

"Actually, I don't know him that well. He eats at Serendipity almost every day so there must not be anyone at home to cook for him. I heard he got a divorce several years ago."

"Do you know his ex-wife?"

Marci shakes her head. "If I ever met her, I don't remember."

"Did you know he and Laura used to be married?"

"What? I can't picture that. Laura is so prim and proper, and Danny is so down to earth."

She had described my attorney and my boyfriend perfectly.

Boyfriend? Did I say boyfriend?

Indeed, I had. I don't know how I feel about that.

CHAPTER 39

THE EMPRESS.

The Empress allows herself to express passion and receive love.

CAL

Danny texted a little later. "Can't talk. Just want to let you know I got Biz to listen to reason. We'll talk more later. See you at 7:00."

I putz around all day, just waiting until time to meet Danny tonight.

Turning off Hwy 92 into Mountain Park I wondered how this community was such a well-kept secret. The curving hilly roads were dotted with rustic cabins and bungalows, yet it was only a few miles from downtown Atlanta.

Danny hears me pull up and comes out to greet me. He kisses me passionately. "I missed you."

"You saw me eight hours ago."

"It seemed like eight years," he says.

"Got anything to eat? I'm starving?"

"Me, too. For you. Sex first. Food second. Talk last."

Tonight, there are lit candles sitting on every possible surface.

I begin peeling off my tee shirt, but Danny stops me. "Slow down," he commands. He lifts the shirt over my head, kissing my neck.

Every cell in my body is begging him to go faster.

He sweeps my hair off my neck and kisses my collar bone. "Relax. We've got all night."

So, I relax. I practice what I preach, to be in the moment and present for our partners. I put all other thoughts and worries and what ifs out of my mind.

He continues to kiss lower and lower. "You smell good."

I have never felt so sexy in my life. I am not in the best of shape, unless "round" is considered a desirable shape. But this man, kissing around my belly button, which is the exact location of my muffin top, declares, "You are beautiful."

After a couple of hours, Danny props himself up on one elbow and nudges me. "You awake?"

All I can muster is, "mmmmmmmmmhmmmmmm."

"This is going to sound really corny, but you know in the movie *Jerry McGuire* when Tom Cruise says to Renee whatever her last name is, 'You complete me?'"

"Mmmmmmmhmmmmm."

"I always thought that was a cheesy line. Until now. Cal, you complete me. You are the missing piece of my life. I have felt more alive and happier today and yesterday than I've ever felt in my life. For so long I've felt my life was over. Now, I feel like it's just beginning."

A knock at the cabin door startles me. Biz again? I tense but relax when Danny says, "It's just Grub Hub. I ordered food for us while you were sleeping. I hope you like grilled chicken salad."

Danny opens the door with the chenille throw wrapped around his waist and hands the man two one-hundred-dollar bills. "Keep the change. Have a good night."

I take a minute to freshen up while he unpacks the food. When I emerge from the bathroom, the dining table is laid with a tablecloth, candles, and flowers. A single red rose stem crosses my plate.

Danny holds out my chair. I ask, laughing, "Tell me again how it is you are single?"

There is a long pause. Too long. I look up. Danny moves the sharp cutlery away from my side of the table before he says, "Technically, I'm not single."

CHAPTER 40

The Eight of Cups advises that you walk away from a relationship that is not satisfying.

CAL

Not technically single? What the hell does that mean?
"I don't understand." I fight to remain composed. "Marci said you'd been divorced for two years. What do you mean you're not single?"

I push back from the food and pick up my clothes from the floor. I can barely hold back the sob lodged in my throat. I was right to be skeptical of a relationship again. I had set myself up for another broken heart.

"Cal, please let me explain. Charlotte left me two years ago. We always had a rocky relationship. She comes from old Atlanta money and her family disowned her when she married a lowly policeman.

"The life she wanted was impossible to maintain on my salary. She met a tech millionaire and moved to Seattle to live with him. She started divorce proceedings before she left, and I was finalizing the paperwork when she was seriously injured in a car accident. The guy left her high and dry. She had a very difficult and slow recovery. I agreed to put the divorce on hold so that she could remain on my health insurance.

"She hasn't signed the divorce settlement. We are arguing over stuff. I've told her she can have it all but the cabin, and she still won't sign. I swear to you this is the truth."

I dressed while Danny was talking. He put his hand on my arm as I'm taking my keys out of my purse.

"Please, Cal. I have never felt about anyone the way I feel about you. I would never have started a relationship with you if I still loved Charlotte. That would not have been fair to you."

He motions for me to sit on the sofa. I sit stiffly in a chair, as far from him as possible. *How did I let this happen again?*

"It took her leaving me and being served with divorce papers for me to wake up and grow up and realize I had no idea what it meant to love someone other than myself. I've spent the last two years figuring out why I was such a self-absorbed bastard (to quote Charlotte) and how to be a better person."

I don't say anything. I'm afraid of what will come out of my mouth. I don't always fight fair.

"I read your book, *Love Hungry*. Right after Charlotte left, Biz tossed it on my desk and told me to read it. It helped. I took responsibility for my part in the failure of my marriage."

I had written that book shortly after Paul and I divorced. When I fell in love with him, I thought I knew what it meant to love someone completely, wholly, unconditionally, and without reservation. I mistook addictive love and codependence for the real thing. When we divorced, I blamed him and laid all the fault for the failure of our marriage at his feet. After a lot of therapy and intense shadow work myself I realized that if I didn't love myself first, I couldn't love anyone else. That book is the story of my journey to loving myself.

One of the messages of my new book is that we are whole human beings. We don't need someone to "complete" us. A partner is extra, the icing on the cake. But certainly not necessary for a happy and fulfilled life.

Danny looks crestfallen. "I had hoped that you and I were moving toward a commitment. A forever kind of thing."

I stand up, keys in hand, and walk to the door. I turn as I open it.

"FYI the book didn't help. You're still a self-absorbed bastard."

I slam the door so hard the glass in it rattles and one of the metal address numbers nailed to it falls off.

CHAPTER 41

The King of Swords is disciplined, using logic in matters of the heart.

DANNY

Screw this. The whole damn world is mad at me. Biz. Cal. Charlotte. I'm sure Marci will be as well once she gets the scoop from Cal.

Laura stopped by the precinct and asked me to grab lunch with her. She looked at me askance when I said, "Anywhere but Serendipity" but didn't ask questions.

"Eagle said she's located Juliet. Are you going to bring her in for questioning?"

"You know Biz is giving me a hard time about this, right?"

Laura pursed her lips. "Since when has a little opposition stopped you from doing what is right?"

"It's more than a little opposition. There are complications."

Laura raised her eyebrows. "Anything I should know about that pertains to my client?" She waited. I was trying to figure out what to say.

"Danny, tell me you didn't."

"Didn't what?"

"Tell me you did not get romantically involved with my client. I saw the sparks fly between the two of you, but I figured you both had enough sense not to pursue it."

She slams her fist on the table when I don't answer. "What have you done? You know I can take this to Judge Carson and get the indictment nullified. Chain of evidence, tainted evidence, the whole nine yards. You'll be ruined."

I can tell she wants to punch me. "Are you going to say anything or just sit there looking like an idiot who is about to be involved in the biggest scandal to hit the Atlanta Police force in years?"

"I admit it. I screwed up." It was harder to admit this to myself than to her.

"Yes. And you screwed my client, too. In more ways than one."

She's shaking her head and mumbling to herself. "I cannot believe this. How could you be so stupid?"

"Stop." I grab hold of her shoulders. "Stop. Please." I cannot deal with one more hysterical woman today.

"I am going to find Juliet. I will get her to confess. Cal will be exonerated."

"And you and your girlfriend will ride off into the sunset together?"

"Not exactly. She ended it."

"Why?"

"I told her about Charlotte."

"She hasn't signed the papers? You're still married?"

"Yes."

"Your life is a mess, Daniel."

"You have no idea."

CHAPTER 42

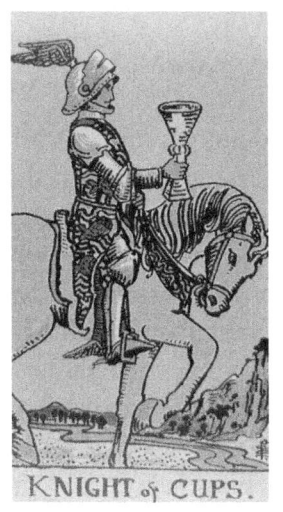

Steady progress unfolds with the Knight of Cups.

DANNY

I miss Cal but I don't miss Cal's erratic behavior. The "one day I love you, next day I hate you" back and forth is exhausting. I don't need that kind of drama in my life.

As a favor to Laura, and because it is the right thing to do, I'm still working with Eagle to bring Paul Davis's murderer to justice. Believe it or not, Biz is on board.

We've had a breakthrough in the case. Biz scrutinizes all lab reports for every case until she is satisfied there are no holes in the data. In this case, she noticed there were traces of cornstarch on all pieces of physical evidence: the shoe, the wine bottle, cup, and the bag. Cornstarch is used to lubricate medical gloves to make them easier to put on and take off.

I went back to the crime scene and dusted again for prints and cornstarch. On a hunch, I dusted the closest bathroom. One partial print from the toilet flush handle came back as a match for Abigail Stewart, aka Juliet Morrison.

I asked Eagle to put a trace on Juliet's credit cards and bank account. I couldn't do it because I didn't yet have probable cause for a warrant. Biz and I were careful to color inside the lines ourselves. As the investigator for the defense attorney, Eagle had slightly more leeway to smudge those lines.

She located Juliet in Marietta. Eagle and I staked out the grocery store where Juliet had used her credit cards several times. She surfaced on the second day. We followed her back to a garage apartment off Hwy. 5.

Armed with new information, I convinced Biz to question Juliet in conjunction with Paul Davis's murder.

We had heard Marci's report of Juliet exhibiting three distinct personalities at her restaurant. The psychiatrist at Summit Ridge confirmed Juliet's diagnosis of Dissociative Identity Disorder.

All three personalities surfaced during the interview. It was a complete circus.

We knocked on the door of her apartment at 8:00 a.m. We wanted her off kilter from the get-go.

CHAPTER 43

The Eight of Swords indicates you are feeling trapped and there's no way out.

DANNY

Juliet opened the door with a robe wrapped around her. We obviously woke her, which was part of the plan. Her voice was soft, as was her expression. "May I help you?"

"Abigail Stewart?"

The panic in her eyes was fleeting. She covered it well.

Her face hardened and in a raspy voice she said, "I'm sorry, you have the wrong house." Juliet moved to close the door.

Biz blocked the door from closing. She pulled out her badge. "Detectives Bizzell and Chan. Atlanta PD. May we come in and ask you a few questions, ma'am?"

"What's this about?"

"May I get your name, ma'am?"

"Maureen. I said there is no one here by the name of Abigail." She pushed harder on the door. Biz's steel toed boot didn't budge.

I spoke up. "As Detective Bizzell said, we just have a few questions in connection with a murder that took place a few months ago."

"I don't know nothin' about no murder."

"I understand. I'm sure we can get this cleared up if you'll just answer a few routine questions. It should just take a minute or two. May we come in?"

Juliet stepped back. She sighed heavily and gestured to the sofa. "Have a seat."

She sat in a recliner chair facing the sofa and lit up a cigarette. The ashtray on the table next to the recliner was overflowing with cigarette butts.

Juliet coughed. It sounded like she had smoked for years.

"I told you those things would kill you."

"Shut up, Darryl."

Biz and I didn't dare look at each other. One of us would have laughed out loud and the other would have quickly followed suit.

"So, Maureen, you don't know Abigail Stewart?"

Juliet shook her head and stubbed out her cigarette. She lit another one.

"How about Juliet Morrison?"

Juliet went into a coughing fit that wouldn't stop. Biz went into the adjoining kitchen and got a glass of water.

Juliet drained the glass, dropped her cigarette into it, and lit another.

With the cigarette in her mouth dropping ash on her clothing and the chair she mumbled, "Nope, never heard of her."

Biz and I stood up. "Thank you, ma'am, for answering our questions." I propelled Juliet toward the door while Biz pocketed the glass with Juliet's fingerprints on it.

"Sorry to bother you. Thanks for your cooperation."

Biz called a friend in the Marietta PD and asked him to keep a unit parked on the street near Juliet's house for the next few days.

On the way back to the precinct we dropped the glass and cigarette butt at the lab and put a rush on the results.

CHAPTER 44

The High Priestess is connected to her divine guidance and sacred wisdom.

CAL

I miss Danny. Or do I? Maybe I miss the man I thought he was.

"See, Marci, this is exactly the reason why I avoid dating and relationships. The men my age have too much baggage."

"Why not date someone younger? Gen X men don't have all the hang ups of Baby Boomers."

"I have nothing in common with a man who was not born when the Beatles debuted on Ed Sullivan."

"Is it really such a bad thing that he didn't tell you he was technically married? He's in the midst of a divorce. The ex-wife won't budge. It's kind of legit that he didn't tell you right away."

We are sitting at my kitchen table. She has brought over healthy zucchini muffins from Serendipity. I am slathering them with cream cheese icing.

"How can you take his side in this?"

"There are no sides. Take your emotions out of it. What would you counsel a client to do in the same situation?"

Marci is right. I can't think straight about the situation because I am too emotionally involved.

After Marci leaves, I go upstairs to the little sanctuary I created in my closet. It is my holy and sacred space.

The depression I've experienced while awaiting trial has robbed me of the desire to do anything but binge eat and be a couch potato. I should know better. Prayer and meditation keep me grounded and centered.

I light a candle and choose stones for meditation. Sunstone. It is a beautiful shimmery peach-colored stone that carries the energy of empowerment. And carnelian. A deep orange-red stone with the energy of passion, joy, and vitality.

Everyone has their own sacred prayer rituals. This is mine.

I sit for a while listening, connected through intuition to a divine power. The answers come. I open my eyes. I know what I need to do.

I hear my phone ringing downstairs. I pick it up just as Laura is leaving me a voice message.

"Cal, can you come to the office? There have been some new developments. Danny and I need to meet with you immediately."

Perfect.

CHAPTER 45

WHEEL of FORTUNE.

Representing the cycles of change, the Wheel of Fortune indicates a turning point is near.

CAL

When I arrive, Laura, Eagle, Danny, and Detective Bizzell are seated around the table. Laura pulls a chair out for me beside her. I am seated across from Danny. He doesn't acknowledge me.

Laura goes into great detail about the theory Danny and Eagle have pieced together with Juliet in the role of murderer. I look at Danny. He is still not looking at me.

I smile at Detective Bizzell. "Thank you."

"You're welcome, Dr. Cassidy. I must say, Danny has been your biggest advocate. If it weren't for him, we wouldn't have uncovered any of this." Danny's face is blank. No emotion. Not love. Not hate. Just blank.

"So, the next steps will be to take this to the prosecutor, right. Then he'll drop the charges against me?"

"We have a working theory. We don't have proof. We can't take a theory to the prosecutor."

"Would this theory convince a jury I'm innocent?" I look to Laura for the answer.

She shakes her head. "I'm sorry, but no..."

Danny speaks for the first time. I'd forgotten how much I love his voice. "We have strung together bits and pieces that are plausible, but we don't think it outweighs the evidence against you.

"The jury will probably start with a presumption of guilt because of the extensive press this murder has received. We know we keep harping on the evidence, but there just isn't any that points in any other direction than yours."

"However," Detective Bizzell interjects, "we have put a plan in motion that we hope will elicit a reaction from Juliet that will lead to a confession."

I waited for more of an explanation. "That's all we can tell you for now. Be patient."

Danny left the conference room first and I made a hasty exit afterwards to catch him.

"Hey, Danny." He paused and turned around. Still no emotion in his face. Just blank.

"Can we grab a cup of coffee and talk?"

CHAPTER 46

PAGE of SWORDS

The Page of Swords brings a fresh perspective to an old situation.

DANNY

When she walked into the conference room at Laura's office, I avoided her gaze. Just seeing her and hearing her voice brought back the memories of our first night together.

Cal isn't conventionally beautiful, but to me she is the most desirable woman I've ever met. Our chemistry was electric but one question I have for myself is why am I attracted to someone who is so emotionally volatile?

I posed that question to Steve the other day.

"This would be the forbidden woman with whom the relationship would be inappropriate?"

"One and the same."

"Remember I said if you are feeling a strong attraction to someone, you need to ask 'why'."

"That's what I'm asking you, Steve. Why am I attracted to someone who is so emotionally unstable?"

"I don't think you are attracted to her because she is unstable. I believe you are attracted to her in spite of it. Let's take a closer look. Can you tell me who she is?"

"Confidentially, it's Caroline Cassidy."

"Ahhh." Steve goes silent for a moment.

"Have you read any of her books, Dan?"

"One. *Love Hunger*."

"The latest book she wrote, *The Shadow Knows*, has a lot of her childhood history and background in it. It's not pretty. What was her last outburst about?"

"When I told her that Charlotte and I were not yet divorced."

"Ahhh." I hate it when Steve does that.

"So, a woman you had several sexual encounters with, a woman who thought you were single, got upset when she found out you are still married. Is that right?"

I hate it when Steve does that.

CHAPTER 47

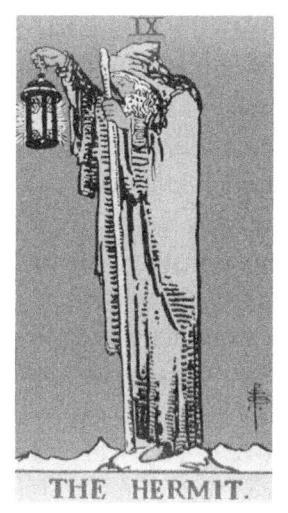

The Hermit is alone but knows there is wisdom to be found in solitude.

DANNY

There is a coffee shop in the Grant building where Laura's office is located. I bought us both a coffee and we sat at a table in the back.

Cal began, "First, thank you for what you've done. Finding Juliet and putting all the clues together."

"Sure."

"Second, I want to apologize for walking out on you and for what I said. I had no right to say that. I don't know you well enough. And what I've experienced of you is that you are neither self-absorbed nor a bastard."

I didn't say anything. It was apparent she had more to say. And there was more I wanted to hear.

"There are certain emotions that trigger cataclysmic responses in me. When I feel I am betrayed, or when I feel rejected, or when I perceive someone is not being honest with me, I have a difficult time maintaining composure.

"Notice I said, 'when I feel' and 'if I perceive.' Because my feelings and perceptions are filtered through my life experiences starting in childhood.

"You once asked why I became a psychologist, and I told you a very safe and watered down version."

She takes a deep breath, like she is preparing for a long dive underwater. "My mother was a very angry woman. She was angry mostly at my dad, who left when I was six. I was the target for my mother's expression of anger, and I have the scars to prove it. Physical and emotional. I still get triggered by perceived rejection. My immediate reaction is, 'I'll leave first before he leaves me.'

"I am not excusing my behavior. I'm apologizing for it. I have difficulty trusting that someone I love won't hurt me. I overreact. I am sorry I overreacted with you."

Cal takes both of my hands in hers. "If we can try again, I promise to do better. To be better." She smiles, hopefully.

"I am a work in progress."

Her beautiful face is full of love and hope and faith.

It occurs to me that I had expected a psychologist to have better mental health. I expected someone with her training and experience to navigate the ups and downs of life with more expertise and less drama.

She is waiting for me to say something. I know what she hopes I will say, but I cannot.

"Cal, I don't think I can make you happy. I'm sorry."

I can tell she is stunned. Her eyes immediately watered and tears stream down her face.

"I understand," she says softly.

Leaving the building, I glance through the window into the coffee shop. Cal is sitting as still as a statue, shoulders slumped, her face in her hands.

I know I've done the right thing. It is better for both of us.

So why does my heart feel like I just smashed it with a sledgehammer?

CHAPTER 48

Leaving turbulence behind and transitioning to calmer waters is the message of the Six of Swords.

CAL

Jury selection starts one month from today. I haven't been sleeping well. I'm scared. No, I'm petrified.

I call Laura every day. "Be patient," she says. "The wheels are turning."

It doesn't appear the plan to get Juliet to confess has worked. I am really going on trial. I will spend the rest of my life in jail. I don't even know how to mentally prepare for this.

Marci has been bringing me meals and spending more time with me. I don't want to leave the cottage. People stare at me everywhere I go. With the trial approaching, my picture, along with Paul's, is plastered all over the local media.

Today Marci shows up with the top down on her baby blue VW convertible. There is a picnic basket in the back seat. "Let's go. We're taking a drive into the mountains."

North Georgia is beautiful. It is the foothills of the Blue Ridge Mountain range, and the area is dotted with clear lakes and streams. We drove to Helen, a little Bavarian-style village. We shop and go to a winery for a wine tasting. No one recognizes me. No one is staring or whispering behind my back.

"This is nice. I needed this." I was sitting outside the dressing room while Marci tried on clothes in a small boutique.

The salesclerk made small talk. "How are you ladies doing this gorgeous day? Having some fun?" It all felt so normal. I hadn't experienced anything resembling normal in months.

A rogue thought crossed my mind. *What if I ran away, far away where no one knows me? Could I get away with it?*

How do people do that? Disappear, I mean. I've had some experience with it. Over twenty years ago my only daughter, Eve, ran away. I was married to my first husband, John, at the time. We paid private investigators tens of thousands of dollars to find our daughter, but they never did. It is the single most shattering event in my life. I think about Eve every day and send love to her, wherever she is. I refuse to think she is not safe and happy somewhere.

Marci and I are sitting by a small stream under a tree. I lay back on the blanket after stuffing myself with one of Marci's famous muffaletta sandwiches.

"You can't be serious," Marci said when I broached the subject with her. "You'd be a fugitive for the rest of your life."

"Being a fugitive is better than being incarcerated for the rest of my life or worse, dead."

"Laura hasn't said anything about progress with finding Juliet?"

"They've located her, but so far, no confession. Danny hasn't said anything?"

"We don't speak that often. He still comes to Serendipity but avoids me."

"Marce, I'm scared, and I don't know what to do. I don't think Laura can convince a jury of my innocence."

"Whatever you do, you know I will support you and help you."

"You can't help me. That's aiding and abetting a criminal. I need to do this myself."

CHAPTER 49

The Six of Cups signifies moving from hardship to harmony.

CAL

On the drive home I called Laura. She does not have any updates for me. "Be honest with me. What kind of chance do you have of winning this trial?"

"We're going to do our best. Hang in there."

That's your best? Your best does not keep me out of jail.

We have the radio tuned to a news & traffic channel as we sit at a dead stop on I-285. I make a mental note to research small towns without major interstates. I hate traffic. Maybe somewhere out west with wide open spaces like Wyoming. Or would New York City be a better place to disappear? I could hide in the midst of eight million people.

"Breaking News in the murder of Paul Davis in five minutes after Drive Time Traffic Report."

Marci reaches to turn off the radio. I stop her. "I want to hear this." The wait is interminable. All of a sudden, I don't care about the traffic. Just give me the news.

"Shocking news today as another suspect has been identified in the murder of Real Estate Developer Paul Davis. Police sources confirm DNA found at the scene matches a former lover of Davis's. The trial of Peachtree College psychology professor and author Caroline Cassidy was scheduled to begin September 5. Stay tuned as we bring you more updates."

I burst into tears.

CHAPTER 50

JUDGEMENT.

Releasing Judgment as we accept our past allows us to follow the call to spiritual awakening.

CAL

I am shaking as I walk up the stone steps of my cottage. Marci takes my arm to steady me.

Does this mean I'm free? Why hasn't Laura called me? I sent a text to her.

Marci sits for a while on the porch with me. "I can't believe it's almost over." I make our favorite cocktail, a gin & tonic with a splash of St. Germaine. We sip and rock together as the sun sets through the trees.

I can finally breathe. It feels as if I've been holding my breath for the last three months. I inhale the pungent fragrance of the gardenia bushes beside my front door.

As dusk falls, Marci leaves to touch base with the dinner chef at Serendipity. I go inside but I leave the door open to enjoy the fragrance of the flowers.

I pour another cocktail and I contemplate the damage to my reputation as a psychiatrist, a professor, an author, and a healer. Is it reversible? Or will my life story always be tainted by, "once accused of murder."

I want to call Danny and celebrate with him. No. He has made it clear he doesn't want anything to do with me.

Why hasn't Laura texted back?

I walk into the living room. Startled, I dropped the drink. Shards of glass scatter all over the brick floor.

"Juliet!"

"Hello, Dr. Cassidy." There is a wild light in Juliet's eyes. Her pupils were pinpoints. *She's on something. Keep her calm.*

It occurs to me that I may not be dealing with Juliet. It could be Darryl or Marlene.

Juliet is holding a gun in her hand. She is wearing purple surgical gloves.

"Juliet?"

"She's indisposed."

"Are you Marlene?"

"No, she died of lung cancer last week. I'm Mandy."

"Mandy, it is nice to meet you."

Juliet/Mandy looks at me like I'm an idiot.

"Really? You think this is going to be a pleasant experience? I'd rethink that if I were you. It's time for you to confess to Paul's murder and then kill yourself. How pleasant do you think that will be, moron?" The contempt with which she speaks is palpable.

"Those stupid pigs came to my door last week and yesterday, too. A cop car has been parked on my street for days, spying on me.

"It is time for you to write your confession, about how you killed poor Paul to exact revenge for his cheating, lying ways, and then swallow some pills." She takes a plastic packet of pills from her hoodie jacket and tosses it. "Catch!"

Without thinking, I caught the packet.

"Now your fingerprints are on the package of pills. Just like they were on the package of cyanide that killed Paul." She clicked her tongue and shook her head. "Tsk, tsk, tsk. You really are too trusting, Cal. Or maybe you're just stupid."

She waves the gun and motions me to sit on the sofa. Shards of the broken cup pierce my feet. "Ouch! Hey, can I just…"

"Shut up," Juliet pushes me to the sofa. The floor was slippery with blood from my injuries, but the brick floor is quickly absorbing it. Juliet closes the front door and locks it. She sits on the chair by the door, opposite the sofa.

"When Abigail started seeing Paul it was so easy to fool you. She mimicked Paul's voice, 'Hey, Callie, listen, I need to meet the developer over in Grant Park to go over the floor plans for Park Side. I don't know what time I'll be home. Don't wait up.' We made fun of your stupidity.

"Everything was perfect until you went psycho on us. Throwing rocks through the windows. Egging his car. Coming to Abigail's office and bashing in our windshield. Paul dumped Abigail just to get you off his back. And I had to listen to that bitch whine about it for months." She cocks the gun. "You're gonna pay for that."

This can't be happening. This can't be how it ends.

"I can't believe how easy it was to make it look like you killed Paul. You never missed the cup and the bottle of wine I stole from you and left at his house." She laughs. "Juliet really wanted to take the Manolo Blahniks with her after she killed Paul, but Darryl and I wouldn't let her. It made such a nice tableau we couldn't bear to spoil it."

A loud knock at the door startles me.

"Get rid of whoever that is," commands Juliet, "or I will kill them too."

I move like a zombie to the door, leaving a trail of blood. I open it a crack.

Danny is standing on my front porch with a bouquet of wildflowers in his hand.

"Hey," he says softly. "Can I come in? I want to talk about the other day." Danny pushes on the door; I wedge my bleeding foot in the doorway and meet his push with resistance.

"Danny, it has been a long day and I have a horrible headache. I'll see you tomorrow. Bye." I try to close the door but can't. Danny pushes harder. My foot is being crushed between the door and the doorframe. Juliet's gun is shoved between my shoulder blades.

"Danny, please, I'm really tired. Not tonight. Tomorrow, I promise."

I know there is no tomorrow for me. But I will not let this madwoman hurt Danny.

"Hey, you're bleeding." He rams the door open, and I stumble back. Juliet points the gun in his face.

CHAPTER 51

The Queen of Wands is powerful, confident, and courageous.

CAL

"Detective Chan, we meet again." Juliet sneers. "Under slightly different circumstances, though." She waves her gun. "I was hoping you'd give up and leave but you are such a persistent pain in the ass."

She motions him to the wooden rocking chair she had been sitting in. "Callie," her voice dripping with venom, "be a doll and zip tie the good detective's hands and feet." Juliet pulls a packet of plastic zip ties from her hoodie pocket and tosses them to me. "Make sure they are tight. No tricks or games."

I tie Danny's hands to the arms of the rocker. My hands are trembling and I realize I've zipped his hands too tight. The ties are cutting into his wrist. "I'm sorry," I whisper.

"His feet, too." I kneel and do as I am told. I look at his face and realize it is this face I want to spend the rest of my life with. Danny winks at me.

He's dissociating.

I try to reason with Juliet. "Listen, this is between you and me. Don't involve him in this. Let him go and I'll take your pills. You don't want to kill a police officer."

Once I say it, I realize how ridiculous it is. Of course, she has to kill Danny, too. He is a witness to her confession.

"Oh, but I do want to kill Detective Chan. Because he has greatly annoyed me this week. I just wish his little bitch partner was with him. No matter, I'll get her, too."

She moves toward Danny and raises his pant leg. She removes his back up gun.

Dammit, that was the only chance I had to get us out of this alive.

Juliet pockets her own gun and twirls Danny's Beretta around her finger. "This is getting better and better! Let's see, the headlines will read, 'Police Detective, that's you,'" pointing at Danny, "killed with his own gun by a suspect." She swings the gun around, "That's you."

She gives me a shove that sends me sprawling on the floor.

"Juliet," says Danny, "don't…"

"SHUT UP! My name is Mandy!" She throws a roll of duct tape at me. "Put some tape over that idiot's mouth before I blow his head off."

I catch the duct tape and motion to my desk. "Can I just get some scissors to cut the tape?"

"NO!" roared Juliet. "Do you think I'm stupid?" She smacks me so hard on the side of the head with Danny's gun that two small cuts open on my temple and cheek. I feel a trickle of warm blood and am faint from the blow.

"That gun is loaded, you idiot!" Danny shouts. Juliet racks the gun and places it under Danny's chin. "Not another word," she says between clenched teeth.

Juliet yanks open the drawer of my desk and retrieves a pair of scissors. "Cut a piece of tape and put the scissors back on the table. If you try anything, I'll kill you first and then him."

I place a four-inch piece of tape over Danny's mouth. I try again to reason with her.

"Mandy, I can see you are in a great deal of pain. I want to help you. I am so sorry for hurting Abigail six years ago." I adopt a soothing tone of voice and assume a non-threatening posture.

"Pain?" shouts Juliet. "You don't know the pain we've felt, you privileged little snot. Abigail found the love of her life and you ruined it. She was going to marry him until you interfered and then he met that Russian trollop and she sunk her claws into him."

She picked up the scissors and stabbed the coffee table each word. "Little" (stab) "Russian" (stab) "Whore" (stab).

I wince with each scissor strike. Spittle pools on the table.

"I am sorry," I said softly. Juliet turns to me with the scissors gripped tightly in one hand and Danny's Beretta in the other hand. "You're going to be a whole lot sorrier very soon."

"Killing me or Detective Chan won't solve anything. Let's stop this before anyone gets hurt."

"You don't get it, do you? Are you really this dense?" Juliet broke into peals of laughter. "You stupid fool. Juliet said you told her, 'There is transformational power in loss' and 'Pain is the portal to self-awareness.'"

She holds the point of the scissors to my neck. I feel the sharp tip pierce my skin and another warm trickle of blood.

"You were wrong. You know what our 'portal to self-awareness' was? Our moment of transformation? When we stabbed that cheating lying SOB in the eye with YOUR high-heeled shoe."

The timer on Juliet's watch chimes. "So, I am creating my own reality. And yours. I want you to watch the detective die. It's very transformational. We watched Paul die and you're right—we felt very powerful as he lay there twitching like a marionette. After the detective dies, you'll swallow some pills and then I'm going to cut out your tongue because you are full of nothing but lies."

Dazed and bleeding, I bend over and vomit on the floor. Juliet aims Danny's gun at his forehead. I sit on the floor and wipe my mouth. I look at Danny's face for the last time.

I hear the shot. "NO!" Blood splatter and brain matter rained down on me. I close my eyes, knowing my own death is moments away.

"Cal, Cal!" I hear a familiar voice behind me and heavy steps on the stairway to the loft. "Are you OK? Dr. Cassidy?"

Disoriented, I open my eyes. Juliet is crumpled on the floor with a large pool of blood discoloring the brick around what is left of her head. Danny is sitting upright in the rocking chair. Unharmed.

Danny cocks his head and winks at me. *What the....?*

I hear the voice again, faintly, and the squawk of a walkie talkie, "Get an EMT in here stat. Dr. Cassidy is in shock and losing consciousness."

I see Biz (*Biz? Where did she come from?)* rush past me toward Danny.

She releases Danny's hands and feet from the zips and pulls the tape from his mouth.

"You good, partner?" Danny uses his tee shirt to wipe the blood and brains from his face. "Never better, Biz. You get all that on tape?"

"Audio and video. Doc's in the clear." She nods her head in my direction.

Danny stands up, stumbling slightly from his legs being tied so tightly to the rocking chair. "Let's get her to the sofa."

Biz takes one side and Danny takes the other. I groan and stir as they lay me on the sofa. I wake with my head cradled in Danny's lap. He is gently wiping my face with a cloth. There are bandages on my temple, cheek, and neck. There is a blood pressure cuff around my arm and an EMT at my side. "Blood pressure is stabilizing. She'll be ok but we are transporting her to Grady. She needs a couple stitches in that neck wound."

"Did I see Biz? Is Biz here?"

"Right here, Doc." Detective Bizzell kneels on the floor beside the sofa.

"You were in my house? How did you get in here?"

"Climbed through the upstairs window." Biz is solemn. "We had to get a confession from Juliet or you were headed for Life Without Parole."

The EMTs came in with a stretcher. "CIS is on its way. Captain Kim and Chief Williams are outside."

The light is beginning to dawn. "Wait a minute." The EMT shakes her head, but I say firmly, "No, give me a minute, please."

I look at Danny and Biz. Despite two hits to my head, one stab wound dangerously close to my carotid artery, and brains and blood in my hair and all over my face, I am beginning to put two and two together.

"YOU USED ME AS BAIT TO CATCH A PSYCHOPATHIC KILLER. THAT WAS YOUR FREAKING PLAN? What kind of people are you?"

Biz has the nerve to laugh.

I'm not finished. "How dare you? You tortured me for months trying to pin Paul's murder on me. Then you pretend to make all nice just to set me up as bait to catch the real killer. She could have killed me! She stuck a pair of scissors in my carotid artery!"

Biz gently touches the bandage on my neck. "As a doctor, you should know this is about a quarter inch from where your carotid is located."

She's right but I'm angry with her anyway. "At least your aim is good."

"I could've gotten her a few minutes sooner if your damn head had not been in the way. And you're welcome."

A blue and red glow lit up the yard. "CIS is waiting," says Biz. "Get her to Grady, you go with her. I'll handle things here."

CHAPTER 52

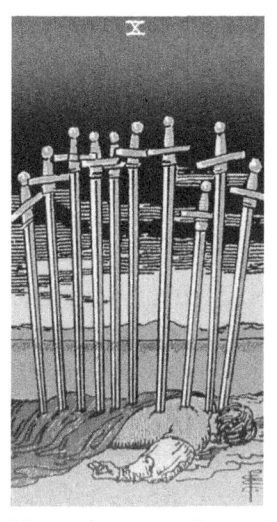

The Ten of Swords reminds us the cycle of darkness and pain leads to transformation.

CAL

The ride to the hospital was short. Tucked into a bed in the ER, I am still shaking with fear.

I hear subdued whispers outside the curtain. Danny's voice, Laura's voice, and a couple of male voices I don't recognize.

A doctor parts the curtain and I smile in recognition. "Hey Kat. I heard you were Chief MO here. How's it going?"

Katherine Hao, MD, Chief Medical Officer of Grady Hospital laughs. "You're lying on a gurney in my ER and you ask how I'm doing?" She gives me a hug. "Quite a few rough months you've had. I've followed things on CNN.

Sorry to hear about Paul." She listens to my chest, watching the monitors attached to my extremities.

"Here's what we're going to do. You've received quite a shock tonight and you're still a bit tachycardic. Your blood pressure is low, and I want a peek at your head wounds. I'm ordering an MRI and then we'll send you upstairs for the night. A nurse will be in to give you a few stitches in your neck."

"Completely unnecessary, Kat. I'm fit as a fiddle." I stand up and promptly faint. Laura pokes her head through the curtain, "I should have warned you that was going to happen."

"Oh, I was prepared for it. You should have seen her in med school. Her nickname was "Dr. Flora" because she hit the floor at least once a week."

An hour later Danny opens the door to my hospital room. He has take-out bags from Serendipity.

"Marci brought this by. She is chomping at the bit to see you. Shall I let her in?"

"Not yet. How could you and Biz use me as bait like that? Juliet could have killed me." I am still disoriented. I'm not sure I'm expressing the full extent of my fury.

"We were out of options, Cal. We had to make the circumstances credible for Juliet."

"Why didn't you warn me?"

"Because you wouldn't have been believable as a captive. And then she would have killed you."

"But you couldn't be sure when she would show up."

"You and Juliet have been under surveillance for a week. The breaking news story about another suspect was planted. A portion of the money you paid Eagle went to the News Director, who is a friend of hers. We knew it would flush out Juliet and force her hand.

"You were never in any danger." Danny squeezed my hand.

"Oh yeah? How were you going to save the day, Mighty Mouse, all duct taped and zip tied to the chair? What if Juliet had decided to just shoot us both in the head instead of playing her mind games? What if Biz had fallen out of the tree climbing into my second story window and broken both her legs? WHAT IF BIZ HAD MISSED?"

The alarm on the machine monitoring my vital signs goes haywire. A nurse scurries into the room. She looks pointedly at Danny. "Sir, you are going to have to leave now."

Danny flashes his badge. Yolanda snorts.

"I don't care who you are, Mister, you cannot disturb my patient. Get out or I'll call security."

I look at the nurse's nametag. "Yolanda, I'm OK and Detective Chan is fine. Dr. Hao is a friend of mine. You can check with her and confirm that Detective Chan can stay."

Yolanda pats my hand. "Dr. Hao has already alerted the station that we have a VIP guest on the floor." She glances at Danny and then back at me. "Are you sure he can stay?"

"Yes and thank you for such good care."

Nurse Yolanda leaves, scowling at Danny. "Watch yourself, Detective."

"If I ever need a bodyguard, I'm calling Nurse Yolanda." I ask again, "Danny, what if Biz had missed?"

"She's a trained sniper. She can hit a target dead center at 800 yards. She did tell me, though, if it came down to it, she would have shot straight through you to kill Juliet to save me if you hadn't moved out of the way at the last minute."

"But that doesn't...."

Danny lays a finger across my lips. "I knew Biz was upstairs with her rifle trained on Juliet. And yet I was terrified that something was going to happen to you. Is your offer still open for us to start over?"

This is the face I want to wake up to every morning.

"Has Charlotte signed the papers yet?"

"No. I'm working on it."

"Work harder. Get that settled. Then, yes, we can start over."

I yawn. The valium is kicking in and I am fading fast. "Can you let Marci in now? I'll just say goodnight to her and let her go home."

I opened the food bag. Bless Marci's heart. I twirl a huge ball of spaghetti and dip it in sauce.

CHAPTER 53

KING of PENTACLES.

The King of Pentacles represents a healthy masculine energy who is generous.

DANNY

I stepped out and found Marci and Laura down the hall talking to Biz. When we got back to Cal's room, Cal was fast asleep with a meatball and a huge glob of spaghetti sitting on her chest, the fork dangling off the bed in her hand.

That's my girl," we said in unison. I put my arm around Marci.

"You guys good?" she asked.

"I think so. We've got a lot to work through."

"Like you using her for bait to catch a murderer. Like you still being married."

"There's that."

Marci continued. "Like her having a hair trigger temper. Like her sabotaging relationships so her worst fears materialize. Like her…"

"Stop. Please. Thanks for being so supportive."

"Oh, I'm rooting for you two. You're Twin Souls. You know, your hearts united in fiery passion."

"Twin Souls? What the hell is that?" I pictured us self-combusting during wild love making, catching the bed on fire, and burning down the cabin.

"It just means she's The One for you and you are The One for her."

I smile. That I understand. I leave the hospital and catch up with Laura in the parking lot.

"How is she?"

"They are keeping her overnight. The chief medical officer is a friend of Cal's and she's running some tests. An MRI. Other stuff."

"Did Biz give the recording to Captain Kim?"

"Yes. I'll file a motion to dismiss first thing tomorrow. After Aaron reviews the tape, I'm sure the charges will be dropped."

Laura touches my arm. "How's your complicated love life going?"

"Help me uncomplicate it. Cal is really important to me. Would you talk to Charlotte?"

"Let me make certain I understand. You want your first wife to talk your second wife into divorcing you so you can marry your third wife?"

"Something like that."

CHAPTER 54

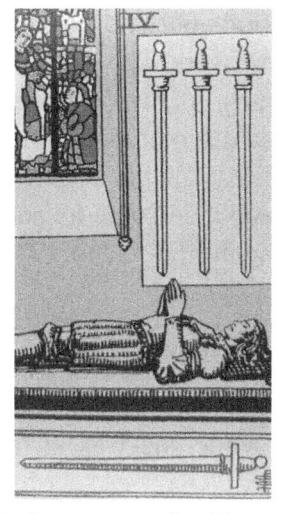

The card of recovery, the Four of Swords indicates it is time for rest and recuperation.

CAL

The following afternoon, I'm relaxing on my sofa while Danny, Marci, Jim, and Gwen hover over me.

"Would you like another cup of tea?"

"Is that pillow comfy enough for you?"

"Here's a book you might like, or would you rather watch a movie?"

"Do you want to take a nap, now?"

Two hours later, I've had enough pampering. I shoo all the mother hens out of the house except for Marci. Danny protests but I promise he can come over later.

I survey the living room. Everything is in order. There are no signs of the violence that had taken place the day before. Biz had a Crime Scene cleaning crew working all night long to erase all traces of broken glass, blood, and Juliet's brain matter. Biz herself sanded the surface of the coffee table to smooth out the gashes where Juliet had stabbed it with the scissors. The coat of varnish was still a little tacky to the touch. A new rug covered the floor where my and Juliet's blood discolored the brick.

It occurs to me that all the busy bees in my hive are people that I love deeply and who love me. Even Biz.

"Biz let me watch the video of last night," Marci confides.

"She did? That seems contrary to police procedure—that's the evidence that will exonerate me."

"Well, she didn't exactly let me watch it. Maybe I sort of took her phone while she was in the bathroom at the hospital and watched it."

Marci starts crying. She holds up two fingers an inch apart. "You came this close, babe. This close."

"I know. I can't believe it myself. I keep reliving that last moment when Juliet's head exploded all over me and Danny." I shudder. "Can you stay with me tonight? I don't think I can be alone tonight."

"We are not letting you stay alone for a while. One of us will be here every night for the next few weeks." Marci pauses. "Unless you don't want Biz to stay."

"No, I think I'd like to get to know her better." If it weren't for her, I would be dead. "She is obviously very important to Danny, so I'd like to spend some one-on-one time with her and get to know her."

For the next week I do nothing but let my friends wait on me hand and foot. They watch over me as I toss and turn fitfully at night and scream and sob in my sleep. One especially difficult night I got up and went into my closet. Sitting in the chair, I began a calming meditation. Peace descended over me as I chanted mantras. When I opened my eyes, Biz was sitting on the end of the bed looking at me in awe.

"That is the most beautiful song I've ever heard. And you are…. glowing. Can you teach me how to do that?"

"Chant or glow?"

"Both."

"Yes. On one condition."

"Name it."

"Will you let me love Danny, too? I don't want to interfere with your friendship, and I realize how important it is to both of you. Is there room in your heart for me, too?"

Biz gives me a fake sigh. "I guess so. Otherwise, he'll mope around and make my life miserable."

CHAPTER 55

The Sun is an indication all is well and offers clarity and understanding.

CAL

I am officially in the clear. Laura gave me the good news a few days ago. After a week of lounging around and binge-watching everything Netflix, Prime, and Hulu had to offer, I'm ready to celebrate.

"Would you like to go to Serendipity?"

"Yes! I've missed going there. Marci says she's got a new Sunday Pot Roast dinner special. I'm starving. Let's go."

I'm pulling on a clean pair of leggings and a fresh tee shirt.

"There's a catch."

I wait.

"Charlotte will be there."

"No. I'm not ready to meet her. I'm still not feeling my best."

"Cal, she's ready to finalize the divorce. But first, she wants to meet you."

"Nope. I can't handle any more drama in my life."

"She insists. She won't sign the papers unless she can meet you."

"What's she like? I'm not in the mood for some demanding, controlling bitch with a chip on her shoulder."

"I think you're going to need one of Marci's valiums."

As we enter the restaurant, I look around to see if I can telepathically recognize the woman Danny had been married to for 23 years. Unexpectedly, I am tackled from the side by a gorgeous brunette who looked like she just stepped out of Page Six.

"Danny, is this our darling Susannah Caroline?"

Never have I ever heard such a heavy southern accent. It sounded genuine and charming. Like old money would sound if it could talk.

Charlotte, wrapped in fur (the real thing) and draped in diamonds (also the real thing), holds me in a vise grip. She smells heavenly, like expensive French perfume. The kind that is $500 a bottle at Neiman Marcus.

I look like a troll next to her in my leggings and tee shirt. I don't care. If that's Charlotte's authentic self, then more power to her and her plastic surgeon.

She takes my face in her beautifully manicured hands, heavy with diamonds and a very large sapphire that puts Princess Diana's to shame. She kisses each of my cheeks.

I am just so happy to meet you, sugar." She guides me to a table and sits me down. "Darlin,' you must be just shattered by all that has happened to you. Bless your precious heart!"

I am speechless. Which is fine because Charlotte is talking enough for the both of us. Danny just sits there looking extremely uncomfortable.

"I'm just so thrilled to meet you, Cal. Can I call you Cal? I've read all your books. You are so smart!"

Charlotte whips her head around, snapping her fingers. "Miss, oh miss," gesturing at Marci. "Honey, could you bring us a round of cocktails. Three Negronis, please."

Marci gives me a "Who the hell is this chick?" look.

"Make that four Negronis, Marci," says a voice from behind.

Laura hugs Charlotte and kisses her on the cheek. "Hello, gorgeous. Good to see you."

Laura gestures to Marci. "Charlotte, have you met Marci, owner of this fine establishment and Cal's best friend? Marci, this is Charlotte, Danny's soon-to-be ex-wife."

"Oh my, the famous Marci! Heavens to Betsy, honey, forgive me for treating you like one of the help. Please, please sit down and join us."

I know Marci. There is no way in hell she is joining this circus. "You'll have to excuse me, but I think I smell a fire in the kitchen."

I glare at her retreating backside. *Thanks for the support, chickenshit.*

Laura removes some papers from her briefcase. "Danny, sign here," she points to the bottom of the paper. "Charlotte, sign here." She turns the page. "Now, here, here, and here."

Danny is staring at Laura in amazement. I see him mouth, "I owe you."

She put the documents back in her briefcase. "Once this is filed, you'll be unhitched and free as the proverbial birds. Give me until 5:00 today."

Charlotte pinches Danny's cheek while looking at me. "I'll bet my daddy's Rolls Royce you're wondering why I fell in love with little ol' Danny, aren't you?"

I fortify myself with a large gulp of the Negroni. "Do tell, sugar."

"Well, I was in my senior year at Agnes Scott when we had a burglary in our dormitory. A burglary! I was scared out of my wits! Danny was the police officer who came to my room to investigate. He was just so cute and charmin'! I could not keep my eyes off him. One thing led to another, and we eloped! My daddy was horrified that I married a policeman. A *Chinese* policeman." She leans over and whispers conspiratorially, "He cut me right out of his will. Not a penny for me. He left it all to that barn-cat third wife of his." She flutters her eyelashes and says pointedly. "Oh darlin,' I did not mean to offend you."

I clear my throat. "No offense taken, Charlotte. That's a lovely story. It has been simply divine meeting you, but I think I'll skip brunch and get a little rest this afternoon. I feel the vapors coming on."

Danny snorts and chokes on his Negroni. I hugged Laura, then Charlotte. When I hugged Danny, I whispered, "I'm ready for dessert when you are, sugar."

CHAPTER 56

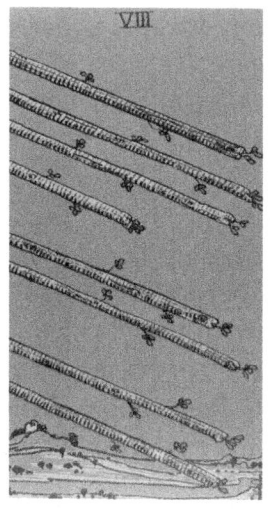

The Eight of Wands suggests new people or new opportunities are coming into your life.

CAL

Danny knocked on my door an hour later carrying a takeout box from Serendipity. "Peace offering. Sorry about all that."

"That was quite entertaining. The best part of that whole scenario was watching you squirm between your first wife, your second wife, and me.

"When I look at Laura, who is beautiful and polished and elegant, and I look at Charlotte who… defies words. All I can think about is, if you fell in love with those two women, what do you possibly see in me? We three women are about as opposite as a pole cat, a gazelle, and a…"

"Circus monkey?"

"Exactly."

"Did my marriages to the gazelle and to the monkey last?"

I shake my head.

"Do you want to know why?"

"Yes."

"This is a horrible thing to admit, and I am not proud of it, but when I married both of those women, I was marrying what they could do for me. They are both from wealthy families." He holds up his hand. "I know—I was a terrible human being. But I will never lie to you, Cal, and that's the truth. And it took a hell of a lot of therapy for me to admit that about myself.

"I loved their status and their money more than I loved them. Obviously neither Laura nor I realized she was gay when we married. We divorced less than a year later.

"After Charlotte left and I read your book, everything came into focus. I learned to forgive myself, love myself, and hopefully, now I can love you the way you deserve to be loved."

I take off my tee shirt. "I'm ready to be loved the way I deserve to be loved, mister. Gimme some sugar."

The months we spent apart made us hungrier than ever for each other. We knew each other's bodies well: where to kiss, where to stroke. It was late afternoon when we finally surfaced after the last round of lovemaking.

"I'm curious. Why is Charlotte acquiescing to the divorce now?"

Danny smiled. "I enlisted Laura's help. They've always been friendly. I didn't get all the details, but I think it has something to do with Laura introducing Charlotte to Senator Markham, whose wife just filed for divorce."

CHAPTER 57

It's time to celebrate with the Four of Wands!

CAL

I am fifteen minutes late meeting Danny for dinner because I couldn't decide what to wear.

"Today is special. Your trial would have started today. Let's celebrate. Dress up, go somewhere fabulous."

We had spent every day and night together since my release from the hospital. Danny decided to retire, and he had months of vacation to take before his last day in early December. I took a leave of absence until the next semester started in January. I'm still not sure if I am going to return to teaching. I'm leaving my options open.

Danny sent a limousine for me. He said Biz needed help wrapping up a case and I should meet him at the restaurant, Moonstone. I don't often eat at fancy restaurants but I've heard the lobster is divine, so I am game to try something different.

Hanging out with Danny at my cottage or his cabin is my idea of perfection. We cook together, clean up the kitchen, and then play games. Scrabble, cards, backgammon; neither of us cares who wins. We are planning a trip out west to Santa Fe and Taos later in the month but in the meantime, we are visiting little mountain towns along the Blue Ridge Parkway. I have never been so happy. I have never been with a man who is so happy to be with me.

I eschew my regular tee shirt and leggings for our fancy dinner. I choose a white silk blouse and black jeans and black stiletto heels. I apologize to the limo driver for making him wait. He is very gracious. "No worries, ma'am," and he hands me a black velvet box. "From Mr. Danny, ma'am. He said to open it now."

Nestled in the velvet box is a silver necklace with the letters C and D entwined. The C and D are set with diamonds. It goes beautifully with my outfit.

As I enter the restaurant, I see Danny sitting in close proximity to a stunning blonde at the bar, having a very intimate conversation. If that had been Paul, or any other man, I would have marched over to the bar, picked up the blonde's drink, and tossed it in my date's face.

I trust Danny with all my heart. He has proven a worthy keeper of my soul. So instead of marching, I glide toward the bar in my sexy blouse and heels.

I know the second I hit a knothole in the bar's oak floors that 4-inch heels were the wrong choice. There is a reason leggings and sandals are my go-to.

My heel catches in the hole and my knee and ankle twist in a way that God never intended. I pitch forward into the blonde. She squeals as her drink drenches her chest and dress.

I picked myself up from the floor and offered an apology. "Oh sweetie, I am so sorry." Danny is laughing so hard he can't catch his breath. I look around. The rest of the bar is laughing, too. Except for Marci, who is rushing toward me, with a bouquet in her hand, for some reason.

"Are you OK?" Familiar faces surround me. Jim. Gwen. Laura. Biz. Several colleagues and friends from the college. A couple of guys in uniform, and a few more dressed in suits like Danny wears to work. I think I recognize Laura's wife, Governor Parker.

"What's going on?"

The blonde giggles. She is mopping her dress with a napkin.

"My dear, we are celebrating you not going to jail today." Danny points to a sign over the bar. It is a four foot by six-foot replica of a Monopoly Get Out Of Jail Free card.

"Except getting out of jail wasn't free!" Everybody laughs. Especially Laura. Laura has laughed all the way to the bank.

I limp over to a table. I'm not sure my knee will ever be the same.

"Cal, this is Darla, Biz's daughter." He gestures to the blonde.

She giggles again. "Nice to meet you, ma'am." Way to make me feel old, honey.

Gwen examines my knee. We went to med school together. She continued with medicine and is now a urologist. She knows where all the body parts are supposed to be, though, and pronounces my knee twisted and my ankle sprained. She goes to get two ice packs from the bartender.

"Marci, why do you have a bouquet in your hand?"

Marci quickly tosses it on a leather banquet seat.

"What bouquet?"

I look at Danny. Who suddenly is on one knee.

"Caroline Cassidy, you are the most fascinating woman I've ever known. Let's spend the rest of our lives together."

He stands up and nods to the crowd. "Old knees. They can only take so much."

He takes a black velvet box out of his pocket.
Crap. I hate that he's doing this in public.

CHAPTER 58

*The Fool embarks on a new adventure,
leaving the past behind.*

DANNY

The look on Cal's face when I ask her to marry me is not a good one.

Did I just blow it again? Are we forever going to be in sync one moment and out of sync the next?

And then she laughs. That donkey bray laugh that I love. She throws her arms around me and knocks the ring box out of my hand.

My girl is all Three Stooges rolled into one.

CHAPTER 59

The Victory Card, the Six of Wands, indicates you are surrounded by people who love and support you.

CAL

What the hell. I love the man. Truly. Madly. Deeply. So what if I preferred it to be a private romantic affair when he asked me to marry him? This is about him, too, not just me.

"Oh, no! Where's the ring?" I knocked it out of his hand when I hugged him.

Darla was the only one in our circle of friends with a young enough back and flexible enough hips to crawl under the bar table and retrieve the ring box.

The ring.

What if it is some gaudy piece of crap like Laura was wearing? I was hoping we could pick out rings together. I wanted a simple band.

I point to the ring box. "Did you pick that out?"
"Yes."
"All by yourself?"
"Yes."
"Biz didn't help?"
"No."
"Marci?"
He shakes his head. "It's a custom design."
I open the box and peek inside. I remove a simple silver band with a small moonstone in the center. The moonstone is flanked by two hearts stamped in the silver.
"Read the inscription on the inside."
I read the words out loud. "My Best & Last."
I hear a few "awwws" from the friends standing around us.
I slip the ring onto my left hand.
"Is that a yes?" He pulls me to him.
"No." Tears are coursing down my cheeks.
"It's a HELL YES."
Everyone claps.
Marci hands me the bouquet. "Ready?"
"For what?"
Biz pushes a button on her phone. Rod Stewart serenades us with an unplugged version of *Have I Told You Lately That I Love You.*
Danny holds out his hand. "Why wait?"
Why indeed.
Danny and I stand before our friends and family, the people we love dearly and who love us back and make our commitment to each other. It is the most holy and sacred moment I have ever experienced. In a bar, no less. "Danny, I promise to love you with my whole heart. You are my best time, my sweetest laughter, and my deepest, truest love. Together we will create our best lives."

Danny takes my hand in his and kisses it. "Cal, I promise to hold your heart in love forever." He winks at me. "You're stuck with me for eternity, baby."

"By the powers invested in me by the State of Georgia, I now pronounce you husband and wife," says Laura happily through tears.

The owner of the restaurant escorts us to a private room where a feast is laid out for our party. Baked Brie, Lobster, Filet Mignon, Scalloped Potatoes, and Brussell Sprouts with bacon and toasted almonds.

"The chef is a friend of mine," said Marci. "I gave her the menu of all your favorite things."

A simple but beautiful two-tier wedding cake sits in the center of the table. It is piped with hundreds of tiny icing pearls, creating a delicate paisley design all over the cake.

My heart is happy. I am basking in the love of my husband, my tribe, and the Universe. Everything really does work out in the end. It is never too late to have the love we deserve.

CHAPTER 60

Your dreams come true with the Ten of Cups. You are in a relationship built on love and respect.

DANNY

I can't remember ever feeling happier than I felt the moment Cal said "yes."

I had hired a symphony quartet to play while we dined. The evening was perfect. The food was delicious. We ate and drank and laughed with our friends. When we danced, Cal's knee still wasn't quite right so we just held each other and swayed to the music, standing in one place.

I never knew I could feel so much love for someone.

The inscription in Cal's ring was something she had said to me a few weeks ago.

We spent the weeks after Cal's release from the hospital talking about our childhoods, our past relationships, our likes, dislikes, goals, and dreams. For instance, I didn't know that Cal will stab anyone who crunches ice in her presence. Or, when she finds a feather, she believes it is an angelic visitation from loved ones. She found out rather quickly that I make disgusting noises when I clear my throat in the morning. She said she could learn to live with it.

We talked about the miracle of our meeting and falling in love.

"I wish I had been your first love." I mused. "I wish we had met sooner."

"We would not be together now if we had known each other sooner. We are two old souls, steeped in shadows, destined to find each other later in life. It is only our pasts that made it possible. We can love each other today because of how the past shaped us.

She continued, "You're not my first love. You are my best and last. You were so worth waiting for."

We said goodnight to our guests shortly before midnight. We didn't have far to go. I rented an Airbnb near the restaurant in Vinings. There was a heated pool off the master bedroom.

Cal emerged from the master bathroom naked. "My knee is still hurting. Take off your clothes and let's go for a swim in the heated pool."

The warm water was an aphrodisiac, not that we needed one. God, I love this woman.

CHAPTER 61

The Page of Wands urges you to be more playful and adventurous.

CAL

For a few days after the wedding, Danny and I sequestered ourselves in a little private cocoon. We turned off our phones except for an hour in the evening when we checked messages. We took short day trips to the mountains, scouring little antique stores and crystal shops for treasures.

Laying by the pool in the warm autumn sun, we dreamed about our future together.

I tried to work on my new book, but I didn't have any interest in the topic. I am no longer single. The creative juices weren't flowing and at one point I closed my laptop in frustration and cursed.

"What would be a better topic for your next book?" We were sipping margaritas by the pool. We were on our second pitcher. "Let me put on my thinking cap."

Danny reached over and picked up my bathing suit top I had taken off to sunbathe. He put it on top of his head, one cup covering his head like an aviator's cap.

"How about, 'My Husband Is The Most Amazing Man In The World and All Other Men Suck'."

I gave him the side-eye.

He took the bathing suit off his head. God, I love this man.

CHAPTER 62

TEMPERANCE.

Temperance asks you to trust in Divine Timing. What should be, will be.

CAL

Too soon it was time to go home and live in the real world. We drove home late Sunday evening. It would be our first night together in our home as husband and wife. We looked forward to celebrating all the "firsts" in the next year to come. We were in our 60s and we were silly newlyweds.

As we turned onto my street, we heard the chirp of a siren and saw flashing blue lights in my front driveway.

A sense of panic and dread washed over me. "Danny, what's going on? Am I going to be arrested?" I can't do this again. "Turn the car around. Don't stop."

Danny pulled into the driveway. "Stay in the car. Let me see what's going on. I know the officer in the car."

A patrolman exited the car and walked around to the passenger door. A little boy about 5 or 6 got out, carrying a teddy bear and a backpack.

"Hey, George, what's up? This your son?"

The officer shakes his head. "Detective Chan, we got a call from Delta Airlines this morning about this little fella. He got off a plane from Mexico City and there was no one in the airport to meet him. He was carrying this envelope. It is addressed to Dr. Caroline Cassidy at Peachtree College. Captain Kim read the letter and told me to bring the boy here."

I had partially rolled down my window and heard what the officer said. Danny motioned for me to get out of the car.

The child is adorably cute, and visibly anxious and scared. I kneel next to him, "Hey little guy. What's your name?"

The boy stared at me. "Azul."

"Azul! That's a great name! I love it. How old are you, Azul?"

"Five."

"Wow, you're tall for your age. Are you hungry? Let's go into my house and see if we can find you a snack."

I unlock the door and Carl rushes me. Marci had fed and watered him while we were gone but he missed his human. Azul giggles and gives Carl a hug. The dog and the boy are about the same size.

I take him to the kitchen and sit him at the table. Carl sits at his feet.

I pour him a glass of apple juice and give him some crackers and peanut butter.

After eating a few crackers he says, "Are you my grandmother?"

I laugh, "Well…"

"Don't answer that, Cal." Danny's face is a mixture of disbelief and anger. He hands me a letter.

Dear Caroline,

This is Azul, your grandson. I need you to take care of him for a little while until I get some things straightened out.

He's a good kid. He loves papaya and pineapple. He likes to look at the stars at night and name the constellations. I'll come get him soon.

His birth certificate is in his backpack. Please keep him safe. He is all I have. Eve.

Slowly I fold the letter. I am sobbing and shaking. Danny asks, "Who's Eve?"

"Eve is my daughter."

"Your *what*?"

I pull a chair beside Azul.

"Azul, is your mommy's name Eve?"

"Her name is Eva. Are you my Grandmother?"

"Honey," I take this little guy in my arms and hug him. "Yes, I am."

A dam breaks inside his little body and he wails. I held him tight, stroking and kissing his hair. No words came out of his mouth as he keens like a banshee for about 10 minutes.

At last, he calms and takes deep gulps of air. He looks at Danny. In between gulps he says, "Are. You. My. Grandpa?

Danny looks at me. I keep my face and eyes neutral. It is up to him. I don't want to influence him one way or the other.

Danny bends down beside my chair envelopes both of us in his arms.

"I sure am, buddy. I'm your Grandpa Dan."

CHAPTER 63

The World signifies completion. There is excitement about new beginnings brought about by your own empowerment and maturity.

CAL

My heart is rejoicing. In one week, I've gained a husband and a grandson. After twenty-six years, I know my daughter is alive. But what kind of danger is she in that she thought the best move was to send her son to me?

I have no clue where to begin unraveling this mystery.

"Azul, do you live in Mexico City?"

"No, we live in Taxco."

I have no idea where that is, other than somewhere in Mexico.

"You live with your mommy?

"Mami and Papi."

He retrieves his backpack, takes out a manilla envelope and hands it to me.

In the stack of papers are Azul's birth certificate and a business card: Eva Castillo, Platero, and a phone number and address in Taxco. A 3x5 card with photographs of stunning silver and gemstone jewelry on the front and information about a gallery and showroom on the back. There is also a photograph of me, neatly cut from one of my book jackets. In a smaller envelope is $10,000 in cash.

I hold the 3x5 card. "Is this your Mommy's work?" Azul nods proudly.

"Wow, this is beautiful jewelry. You must be very proud of your Mommy."

Again, Azul nods and smiles a great big toothy grin. "She's a silversmiff."

"What about your father, Azul? Where is he?"

The grin disappears. "I don't know."

"Oh baby, I am so sorry." I hold him tight, my eyes watering as I consider what this little fellow has been through.

Azul yawns and hugs his teddy bear.

"Hey, let's get some jammies on and make up a bed for you, OK? Does that sound good?"

I ran a bath and gave Azul a quick scrub. He is so tired he is close to falling asleep in the tub.

Danny made the sofa in the loft outside our bedroom into a bed for Azul. He comes into the bathroom and lifts Azul out of the tub. "Come on, buddy, let's get you dried off and jammied up. Grandma and Grandpa are old farts and we need to go to bed."

"Grandpa! You said fart!" Azul breaks into squeals of laughter.

I sit in the rocking chair beside the sofa and Azul climbs onto my lap. He is tall for a five-year-old and gangly in the big puppy way that all little boys are. I revel in the weight of him on my lap and the way he snuggles into my chest, his wet hair soaking my tee shirt.

I sing the lullaby I sang to Eve when she was little. "Rock a bye baby, in the treetop." Azul sings along with me. When I get to the part about "when the bough breaks," he sings it the way I sang it to Eve. "When the bough breaks, the baby will fly, up to the moon and stars in the sky."

Which means Eve has sung our special lullaby to her son. My heart is full of love for this boy and Danny, and full of longing for my daughter, Eve.

He burrows deeper into me and is asleep within minutes.

Danny lifts him from my lap and tucks him into bed with his teddy bear. We both bend at the same time to plant a kiss on his forehead. Azul sighs and smiles in his sleep.

In the bedroom, I crawl into bed in my tee shirt. "What an unbelievable day."

"Yeah, unbelievable," echoes Danny. "By the way, we're even."

"Even? What do you mean?"

"My 'I'm still technically married' thing is cancelled out by your 'I forgot to tell you I have a daughter' thing."

"We both kept secrets from each other," I said solemnly. "Come to bed. I'm exhausted."

Danny was packing a duffle bag. "You want me to stay? I thought you might need some time alone with Azul. He might be more comfortable if I'm not here. I can sleep at the cabin and then come back in the morning."

"Absolutely not. That boy needs some consistency in his life. All he knows is that I am his grandmother, and you are Grandpa Dan. You add a sense of calm and safety that he desperately needs. Please stay."

Danny drops the bag. "Whatever you need. I'm all yours."

I showed him the cash and cards from Eve. "With this card maybe I can find Eve. I can't imagine what transpired for her to put Azul on a plane to Atlanta. She must have been desperate, and I was her last resort.

Danny just nods his head. He is waiting for an explanation.

"I apologize for not telling you about Eve. She ran away when she was seventeen. For twenty-six years I've not known where she is. John and I could not find a trace of her when she left and believe me, we tried. The private investigators we hired never picked up her trail. It was like she vanished into thin air."

My eyes fill with tears. Danny hands me a tissue. I motion for him to give me the entire box.

"It was wrong of me not to tell you. I was afraid of what you would think of me. What kind of person must I be for a child to run away and never again make contact?"

I am bawling like a baby. Danny takes a handful of tissues and wipes my tears.

"Cal, it wasn't all about you. Eve bears some responsibility for this, too. I don't know what you were like so long ago, but I'll bet you aren't the same person now as you were then. We do the best we can with what we have and when we know better, we do better.

"I should have done better then. Eve left because I abandoned her emotionally. Her father and the congregation expected her to be a paragon of virtue and spirituality. The pressure was more than she could bear, and I didn't stand up for her because I was too busy with my career.

I am sobbing so wildly that the bed is shaking. Danny wraps his arms around me and holds me tightly, like he is swaddling a baby.

"And yet, who did she turn to when she was desperate? Who did she trust to care for the person who means everything to her? You. She sent her son to you. She knew you would not abandon him.

He kisses my forehead. "You are a good person. No, you are a *great* person. I've seen you navigate difficulties over the last year that would destroy most people. And you've done it with grace and dignity."

Danny's phone pings with an incoming text. "Earlier I called the Chief of Police in Taxco and asked if there were any leads on Eve. This is him getting back to me."

He reads the text. He does his best to cover it, but I can see his face fall. "No news yet."

"Let me see your phone, Danny."

"This is not definitive. I don't want you to worry."

I snatched the phone from my husband's hands.

Detective Chan, the Taxco police have responded to a break in at the home of Alvaro and Eva Castillo. There are signs of a struggle. The family is missing.

"Well, we know Azul is safe and Eve put him on the plane. I would bet she is safe, too." Danny's words are reassuring.

Danny types into his phone.

"Are you responding to the police in Taxco?"

"No." He types for another minute and then shows me a screenshot. He has purchased three tickets to Taxco on Delta Airlines, one for me, one for himself, and one for Azul. "We are scheduled to leave for Taxco the day after tomorrow. Let's find our daughter."

ACKNOWLEDGEMENTS

You would not be reading this novel without the help of many wonderful people in my life.
My biggest debt of gratitude goes to MJ Hodges, my daughter. She is my greatest joy. When I needed to step away from my boutique so that I could write, she took over and became an amazing Girl Boss and manager.
To my employees who keep the boutique a happy place for people in the community to congregate, thank you from the bottom of my heart. Marci McGee, you are marvelous! You've been with me from the first day I set foot in Gulfport, and I am indebted to you. Ashley Wix, you make this world (and Zaiya) a more beautiful place. Julie Armstrong, you rescue me time and time again and I am so grateful. I am thankful to have such a wonderful crew backing me up.
Marjorie Lewis, you are a brilliant editor and writing coach. You have shaped and improved my writing in ways that no one else could. Thank you for believing in me. To our writing group—John, Debbie, Lauren, Tim, and Robert—thank you for all the suggestions and ideas that have made my novels better.
To my Gulfport Tribe, Margo Dalgetty, Julie Armstrong, and Shirley Baldwin, THANK YOU FOR NOT LAUGHING AT THE FIRST DRAFT OF THIS NOVEL. You gave me some great ideas for improvement. Lisa Taylor, Marilyn Mackey, Dana Garvin, Marci McGee, Nana Hendricks, Vicky Gray, Debbie Bedrick, Tracey Pregon, Shelly Straub—you keep me grounded and accountable.
To my Atlanta Ride-or-Die Tribe, Pam Slappey, Cheri Huff, Cindy Cook, Becky Stanborough, Judy Fuller, Laura Gunter, Pat Berryhill, Diane Simone, Donna Quam, Sue Poole, you know why you mean so much to me. We all

survived and thrived! Becky, thanks for the suggestion to add the Tarot Cards to the story.

To my siblings who have supported me emotionally and financially in all of my endeavors, even the hare-brained ones (there have been so many):

Patricia Harwell, thanks for helping me make Cal Cassidy a little more believable as a psychologist.

Jack Rice, Jr., while my style of writing isn't your "cup of tea" you have always been there for me. Mom and Dad would be proud of you.

Janice Pankey, thank you for your prayers and for being my cheerleader.

To all the fantastic people at WildBlue Press—thank you for making a decades-long dream real.

For More News About Jill Rice And Other Great WildBlue Press Romantic Suspense Books Signup For Our Newsletter:

http://wbp.bz/newsletter

Word-of-mouth is critical to an author's long-term success. If you appreciated this book please leave a review on the Amazon sales page:

http://wbp.bz/mbala

More Romantic Mystery from WildBlue Press

| WildBlue Press, 2016 | WildBlue Press, 2017 | Lost Canyon Press, 2018 |

Janice Boekhoff's Earth Hunters Series embarks on captivating journeyes where ancient secrets reveal timless truths and pave the way to love and faith. These suspenseful blend heart-stirring adventure, romance, and wholesome themes.

In **CREVICE**, Elery Hearst delves into the depths of Arizona's Lost Dutchman's Mine. The quest for her family's legacy transforms into a soul-searching adventure, intertwining her fate with Lucan Milner. Together, they navigate a labyrinth of old wounds and emerging threats, their faith and emotions intensifying amidst the rugged terrain.

CREATED takes us to the lush, mysterious jungles of Costa Rica with Paleontology Professor Travis Perego. His pursuit of a revolutionary discovery challenges the boundaries between science and faith. Teaming up with Lenaia, a woman harboring her secrets, they face the wilderness, their ethical convictions, and their unresolved histories. In their journey, the struggle to safeguard their discoveries is as daunting as their quest for personal redemption.

In **CASCADE**, we meet Geologist Lenaia Talavera, who gets more than she bargained for when she's called to Mt. Rainier to investigate an act of sabotage. Not only is she forced to confront her left-over feelings for her ex-boyfriend—feelings her current boyfriend wouldn't appreciate—but women from the nearby town are disappearing… only to be found dead.

Unraveling these mysteries might not be easy, but it could be the key to a profound renewal of their lives and beliefs.

More Crime Mystery from WildBlue Press

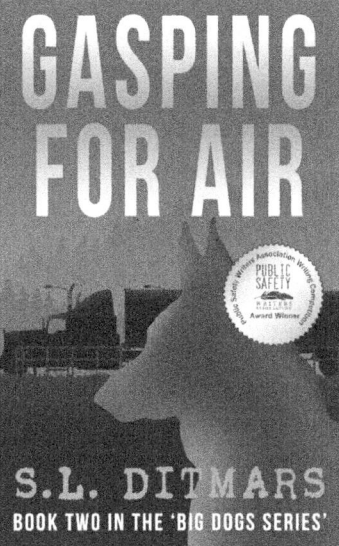

Discover the award-winning *Big Dogs* **series** by S.L. Ditmars, featuring Lieutenant JW North and his elite K9 unit as they take on dangerous criminals. JW and his German Shepherds, including the powerful Ares, navigate through the darkest corners of crime to keep the world safe.

In **BIG DOGS**, JW North embarks on a heart-stopping mission as he seeks justice against a brutal assailant, setting the stage for a high-stakes adventure with the FBI's special task force. The hunt for a serial killer in a Las Vegas hotel marks the beginning of a relentless pursuit of justice.

The suspense intensifies in book two, **GASPING FOR AIR**, where JW, now a U.S. Marshall, and his partner Ben Kellum face the Truck Stop Killer's wrath. Together, they edge closer to capturing a murderer responsible for a string of heinous crimes, racing against time to save the next victim.

With each turn of the page, the Big Dogs series promises intense action, emotional depth, and unwavering loyalty. Join Lieutenant JW North and his K9 partners as they confront evil head-on, proving that courage and companionship are your strongest allies in the battle between good and evil.

Made in United States
North Haven, CT
19 May 2024